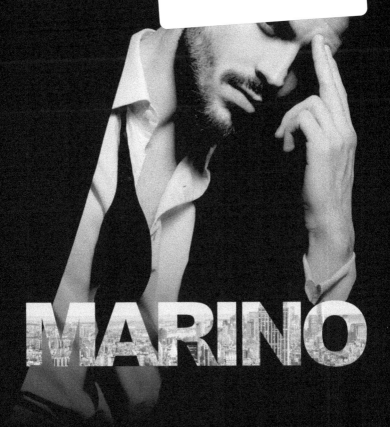

MARINO

SINFUL NEW YORK SERIES BOOK TWO

ADDISON TATE

Marino

Sinful New York
Book 2

Addison Tate

KALEIDOSCOPE
PUBLISHING LTD

Dedication

This is for the baddies who love a battle of wills, a ruthless Mafia boss, and the woman who refuses to break for him. Until she does.

Massimo Marino is ready to fight you, ruin you, and own you...

I never expected my stepfather's sins to cost me my freedom.

One moment, I'm dreaming of a future I actually want. The next, I'm being handed over to a man who doesn't know the meaning of mercy.

Massimo Marino is ruthless, a man feared by many, and now he's my husband. To him, I'm nothing more than collateral for a debt owed. But if he thinks I'll be the obedient, silent wife, he's sorely mistaken.

Yet the more I fight, the more tangled we become. Every glance, every touch, every threat sends my pulse racing with something far more dangerous than fear.

I thought my freedom was the only thing worth fighting for. But when I uncover the truth about the traitor among us, I realize Massimo isn't the only monster at my door.

Now, the real question isn't whether I can escape him, but whether he'll believe me before it's too late.

Authors Note

As with any book I write there will always be a happy ever after, however, to get there we go through a lot of turbulence and trauma.

This book contains some themes that may be triggering and in the interest of putting your mental health first, please scan the QR code below for the full list of triggers.

Translations

Below is a list of the Italian words and phrases used throughout Marino for your reference.

Nonno - Grandfather
Consigliere - Advisor
Capiscio - Understood
Fedeltà Eterna - Eternal Loyalty
Ciao - Goodbye

MARINO

ADDISON TATE

Chapter 1

Massimo

The stench of sweat, blood, and urine permeates the air, mingling with the cries of a broken man. As he begs for his life, I've never felt more alive. I pace around the room, the evidence of his suffering splattered across my clothes.

In hindsight, dealing with this in the office at Aces wasn't a smart idea. I'll need to get a new rug and have the room deep-cleaned to eradicate any traces of him once he's dead. The cost is barely a dip in the ocean, considering how much this man owes me, but it's the inconvenience that fuels every swing of my fist to his face. The crunch of his breaking bones serves as my payment, but we both know that no matter how many bones I break, it will never cover his debt.

Daniele, my cousin Romeo's underboss, lounges on the navy-blue velvet couch on the far side of the room, his arms spread across the back. After the attacks sustained on my family over the past six, or so, weeks, Daniele stayed behind, while Romeo returned to Sicily.

Something akin to discomfort—or possibly judgment —flickers in his gaze when I glance his way, but he shuts it down almost as quickly as it appears. We don't always see eye to eye on how matters should be handled. I am more hands-on and tend to take action, whereas Daniele is more reserved.

Leonardo, my underboss, is away tracking down a runaway housekeeper—Haven—and we've needed all hands on deck. There is bound to be more bloodshed. For one, Elio Morretti, one of the men we believe to be behind the attacks, has gone into hiding and we are still trying to find out who in my own house was feeding him information.

As if all of that wasn't enough, I still have legitimate businesses to run, like my club, Aces, and not so legitimate ones, collecting debts owed to me by men who do not know their limits or abilities. Which is how Alvin Davis has ended up here, tied to a chair, begging for one more chance to repay me.

"I'm sorry, Mr. Marino." Trembling words cut through my thoughts. I turn toward the low-life who's pleading with red-rimmed eyes and tear-soaked cheeks. "If I didn't think it was a sure thing, I *never* would have borrowed money from you," he whines, as if that changes anything.

Smoothing a blood-covered hand over my stubbled jaw, I acknowledge the adrenaline coursing through my veins, sharpening my every move and feeding the chaos coiled in my chest.

This isn't about Alvin anymore.

It's *everything*. The pain I am inflicting on him is an amalgamation of the weeks of pressure, the deaths of many of my men, unanswered questions, betrayal, the loss of thousands of dollars' worth of goods, and the gnawing doubt that we'll never find the people behind the attacks.

Alvin's head rolls forward in defeat and possibly shame. A string of saliva mixed with blood hangs from his mouth, dripping onto the fabric of the chair visible between his legs. I grind my jaw, the sight pissing me off more than it should.

Moving around the room, I stretch out my tired arm, preparing to continue my assault on him. I come to a stop in front of him, the tips of our shoes mere inches apart. Tilting my head, I stare down at him, sizing him up like a predator hunting its prey.

My sudden movement as I reach out makes him flinch. A rush of adrenaline races through me and I don't bother to contain the wolfish smirk pulling at my lips. The power I wield isn't something I take lightly, but it sure is fun watching petty pieces of shit like Alvin cower at my feet.

Grabbing a fistful of his hair, I yank his head back, savoring the startled cry that escapes him. *Pathetic.* His eyes are glassy, but in the depths, I see the terror dancing there. Hell, I feel it as his body trembles in my grip. The fear reflected only fuels the primal, sick thrill that burns through me. It's the perfect fuel for the embers of anger and frustration that have been simmering away since the first attack. I thrive off it and it flows through my body like blood.

With my eyes locked on his, I pull my arm back and watch as he tenses, squeezing his eyes shut like the coward we both know he is. I connect my fist with his cheek. A loud, sickening crack echoes around the room, and Alvin cries out, blood bursting from his mouth and spraying, wet and hot, onto the fabric of my black shirt. He jerks in his chair, gasping for air as crimson paints his lips and gathers on his chin before dripping to the floor below.

"We're at what some might call an impasse, Alvin." I push his head away roughly before releasing him. Circling the chair he's tied to, I adjust the rolled up sleeves of my shirt, straightening them, grateful that my choice in clothing—always black—masks the blood splatters he's covered me in. "You owe me a lot of money, and yet you're telling me that you have no way of paying it back." I rub my hands together, keeping my voice low and lethal. Each word is measured and meant to convey with certainty exactly what is going to happen. "Do you see what my issue is with that? You're not really leaving me a choice here, Alvin."

I step forward, the corner of my mouth lifting when his eyes widen. *This is a high I could live on.* That power, control, the metallic scent, it's all a reminder of the fact that his life is in my hands, and with a snap of my fingers, he could be gone.

He swallows thickly, adjusting his posture as best as he can, given his restraints. "Please, Mr. Marino. There's got to be something—anything—I can do. Something I can give you that will clear the debt." His voice cracks. There's no mistaking his desperation.

Dragging over a chair, I drop into it and lean back with my legs wide and caging in his own. We stare at each other, his eyes wide and desperate. The silence of my pause hangs heavy between us before I say, "There's not much you can give me, *Alvin.*" I spit his name, firing it off of my tongue in disgust.

Does he seriously think that he can give me anything other than his life? Men like Alvin gamble recklessly and not just with their—or in Alvin's case, my—money, but with lives too. *It's predictable.*

There's a brightness in his gaze that I can't wait to extinguish. "Whatever it is, I'll hand it over. No arguments."

I stare down at my blood-covered hand, flexing it as I inspect the tender and bruised flesh with an air of nonchalance. Holding his gaze, I say, "There's only one thing I want from you."

"Anything," he breathes, his voice quiet, but his hope amplified in the silence of my dimly lit office.

With my best poker face in place, I reply, "You can pay me the half a million dollars that you owe me."

Alvin deflates before me, blowing out a heavy breath.

Fascinated, I watch as any hope leaves him. It's like snuffing out a light and being drowned in darkness. Hope is an emotion for the naïve. He's a fool to think there's any chance of him leaving here alive if he can't return to me what is mine *tonight*.

"Mr. Marino, I'm begging you. Surely, we can set up a payment plan or something." His desperation reaches new heights as he attempts to shift forward in his seat, his eyes seeking mine out.

I bare my teeth, sitting forward to rest my elbows on my legs and forcing him to lean back. We're so close that I can smell his fear, mixed with the stench of urine, and I curl my lip in disgust, looking down my nose at him. "This isn't a fucking bank, Alvin. You can't ask for an extension on a loan. The moment you walked into my office and asked for that money, you knew what you were getting yourself into."

I take hold of Alvin's hand, holding out his pinkie finger. A sick, twisted smile spreads across my face. I can only imagine what he must see. Whatever it is, it has him thrashing around, the zip ties binding him to the chair, digging into his wrists and turning his flesh an even paler shade of white. My grip only tightens, forcing his finger to stay still while the rest of him bucks like a wild beast. Not taking my eyes off him, I pull the cigar cutter from my pocket.

"Please, Mr. Marino. I'm sorry. Don't do this. Please," he begs, his pleas falling on deaf ears.

I stand abruptly, my chair falling to the floor with a

soft thud, but I don't pay it any mind. "Unfortunately for you, I can't cash in your apologies and promises. There's nothing that you can do that will stop me taking your life. *That* is the only payment I will accept."

I slide the cutter over his finger, and smirking, I push the sides together. There's a slight resistance at first, but with a practiced pressure, the crunch of bone splintering soon sounds around the room; intense and visceral. It collides with the shallow gasps from Alvin's choked sobs. Something about that sound—discordant, raw, *perfect*—it's music to my fucking ears. Alvin's eyes roll back, his head tilting to the side as his body goes limp.

I step away, admiring the finger on my rug, the steady drip of crimson from the stub on his hand, and the blood seeping into the cream threads. It all adds to the symphony of his pain; of my pleasure.

Lowering into my chair, I wipe the cigar cutter with a handkerchief before pocketing them both. Alvin mumbles nonsensical words, and when I look at Daniele, he shrugs, as in the dark as I am about what he's saying.

Pulling on the front of Alvin's shirt, I force him to sit up straighter and demand, "Come on, Alvin." Slapping his cheek again and again, trying to rouse him, I sneer. "We're only just getting started. This won't be what kills you. This is purely for my own entertainment."

Alvin rolls his head around to look at me, his eyes heavy like he's seeing through me before he blinks and obviously brings me back into focus as fear carves into his expression. He won't make it past one hand, let alone both, and his feet. *Spoilsport.*

"Please," Alvin rasps. "Mr. Marino, please, there has to be something I can give you?" His breaths come out in a spluttered wheeze, his words barely audible. "S-some-one." He winces as the word leaves his mouth, and I'm certain it's not from the position he finds himself in, but that he is about to offer up someone that he has no right to barter with. Firming his resolve, he whispers, so faint I almost miss it, "I can give her to you."

My body stills, the wild energy inside of me calming like we're stepping into the eye of a storm. I circle his throat in a grip hard enough to feel his pulse hammer under my fingertips. "Her?" I echo, my voice dangerously low. "And who the fuck is 'her'?"

I apply more pressure in a silent command for him to speak. "My stepdaughter," he croaks, his voice trembling like a condemned man. The words hang in the air, stark and jagged, cutting through the haze of blood and adrenaline, silencing the promise of his death.

For the first time tonight, I pause.

Chapter 2

Margot

I've been half listening to the news anchor on the TV screen while staring aimlessly at the ceiling, bored out of my mind. It's another rainy Tuesday night in the middle of spring, and I have nothing to do. I can't even go and see my boyfriend, Ethan, because his parents are in town, and as it's been a while since he last saw them, we agreed he would have a solo night with them.

From my spot in the living room, I hear the front door open. A horrified gasp from Josephine, my mother, pulls my attention, and I peek over the back of the couch, while simultaneously burrowing into the old, worn out cushions to keep from being seen. Hushed whispers from Josephine and a more masculine tone that I assume is her husband, Alvin, float through the ajar living room door, but no matter how hard I try, I can't hear exactly what's being said over the sound of the TV.

For a moment, I hesitate, questioning whether I want to know what's being talked about, but my curiosity gets the better of me and I slink over to the back of the couch, my movements sure and practiced. I've spent plenty of evenings sneaking in from being out late with Ethan when we were younger. We didn't get much privacy with our parents around, but as we've grown older and he's moved into his own place, that hasn't been an issue.

Keeping to the wall, I inch my way closer to the door. The light from the hallway beams into the room, and I hold my breath as if I'll give away my position. From here, I can see Josephine and Alvin, her husband. He's slumped against the wall, his back to me.

There's an air of panic and hurriedness unfolding before my eyes. Josephine wraps her arm around Alvin, helping him walk as they move to the back of the house.

When they are out of sight, I move, following in their wake, my eyes trained on their retreating backs as they enter the kitchen. A swirling in my gut tells me something bad has happened, and I need to find out what it is.

Josephine flits around the room like a bird caught in a storm, her feather-lined robe trailing behind her as she mutters to herself. I watch her, the familiar embers of my frustration at her dramatics sparking to life beneath the surface. Regardless of what's happened, I shouldn't be surprised by her reaction. This is typical of her; she panics and flusters until someone—usually me—comes in to fix the mess.

"I can't believe this, Al. This can't be happening."

Her voice is high-pitched and panicked as she replies to whatever news he's told her.

My gaze follows hers, landing on Alvin as he lowers himself into a chair at the kitchen table. I can practically feel the pain slicing through his body. The air catches in my throat, choking me, as I take in the sight of him. His face is bruised, swollen, and bloody, but it's his hand wrapped in a blood-soaked cloth that draws my attention. He holds it tentatively to his chest, wincing as he relaxes against the back of the chair. I force myself to move further into the room, every step stiff and heavy as I scramble to process the scene in front of me.

I might not like Alvin much—we've never seen eye to eye—but nobody deserves to be bleeding and broken like this. *Even him*.

He inhales sharply when his attention jumps to me, a sheepish look covering his features before he rips his gaze away. A sour taste coats my tongue, and a knot forms in the pit of my stomach as I wait for him to speak.

Something has happened, that much is clear.

Staring at him, I try to make sense of what has happened, taking in the extent of his injuries. Did he get into an accident? Or worse, did somebody do this to him? Are they going to come for us next? Is that why Josephine is in a panic? Is he looking at me like that because I'm going to be beaten? A cold rush of unease spreads through my body, leaving me breathless.

I barely catch myself when Josephine's body collides with mine, sending me staggering back a few steps as I try to keep us upright. Gentle sobs wrack her body and, instinctively, my arms wrap around her to offer some form of comfort, my own emotions sidelined for hers, yet again. At this point in my life, I am the parent in my relationship with my mother.

Josephine Dupont was born in France to a farmer and his wife—my grandparents, who I've never met. She moved to America when she was eighteen with a dream of becoming the next Marilyn Monroe. She likes to make out that I'm the reason she never saw that dream fulfilled, but we both know that she was a washed-up actress way before she conceived me with some sleazy Hollywood producer who wanted nothing to do with either of us when he found out she was pregnant.

She pulls back, smoothing my hair back from my face, like she did when I was a child. "Oh, *mon chéri*. I'm so sorry."

Her eyes glisten in the dim lighting, but I don't let the unshed tears soften the edge to my voice. "What are you sorry for?" I ask, skepticism filling my words. Her apologies are about as rare as they are sincere.

Gripping her wrists, I pull them away from my face and put some distance between us. It's hard to think when she's like this.

But we've never had drama in our lives like this before.

This feels different, like there's an obvious air of danger that's threatening to drown us, and that alone scares me. Josephine wrings her hands, staring down at the floor as my question lingers in the space between us.

"What are you sorry for?" I snap again, my focus jumping to Alvin before returning to her. "What's happened?" Familiar gray eyes stare back at me, wide and fearful, before she looks over her shoulder at him.

Alvin clears his throat, scrubbing his left hand over the back of his neck nervously. "It's nothing," he grunts.

Grinding my jaw, I narrow my eyes. "It's clearly not nothing. What happened to you, and why is she in tears?"

Josephine grabs my hand, tugging me toward the table. Her tone is soft and cajoling, but it doesn't fool me. She wants something. They both do, and I'd put any money I might have on it being something only I can do. "Come, have a seat and we can talk about it. Find a solution *together*."

I furrow my brow, taking a step back and forcing her to let go. Her gaze holds mine, but it doesn't feel familiar anymore; she looks broken. *That can't be right.* She blinks, and whatever I thought I saw is shuttered away as her resolve hardens and she turns away to rush across the room to Alvin. They bicker, their voices low and their words indecipherable. And pity, she's tending to his wounds, dabbing at the blood on his face with a white cloth.

"Enough!" I shout, my voice cutting through the chatter and silencing them. "I don't care who does it, but *somebody* had better tell me what the hell is going on."

Alvin covers Josephine's hand with his uninjured one. "It's a done deal, Josie." Resignation coats his words, filling his features and seeping into his body until he's practically slumped over in his chair.

Josephine begins pacing, her distress evident in the way her features are pinched and her arms flail as she cries, "But it can't be." She pauses before a look I've never seen washes through her features. "She's my baby. You can't do this," she screams at Alvin.

Bullshit.

I haven't been her baby since I wore diapers, but this is all part of the show. Josephine is a much better actress in life than she ever was in her career and she's more than prepared to give the performance of a lifetime. Frustration burns through me, swirling with the cloud of annoyance. Not only are Josephine and Alvin in their own little world, having a conversation about something they are yet to share, but whatever it is, it has *something* to do with me. And I want to know. Hell, I deserve to know.

"*What.* Is. A. Done. Deal?" I bellow, drawing their attention to me.

A hint of something that looks as close to remorse as Alvin can offer flashes through his eyes. But he blinks, and it's gone, leaving behind the coldness I'm used to.

Shrugging a shoulder, he drops his attention to his bundled up hand, carefully unwrapping it. "I'm sorry, Margot." *He doesn't sound sorry at all.* "But you're getting married."

Married?

Silence descends on us like a guillotine. Josephine's eyes grow glassy and Alvin's features smooth out with something akin to sympathy as I stand, rooted to the spot in shock.

To Ethan? He's going to propose? Giddiness rushes through me. But we're both so young and I barely have my life together.

Irritation douses my excitement. Why would he tell them before asking me? He knows what our relationship is like.

A million questions run through my mind, and I press my fingers to my mouth as I try to process the appropriate reaction.

I'll say yes, of course. He's the love of my life and we're going to get married eventually.

But why was Alvin beaten if Ethan is going to propose? I brush away the question, choosing to focus on my own happiness.

I roll my lips to keep my grin at bay, but it falls away the second I look at Alvin. My chest tightens and his cold eyes hold mine, the truth skating down my spine like ice water.

Ethan isn't proposing.

"And who exactly am I marrying?" I demand, folding my arms across my chest. My bravado is a front for the uncertainty about whatever Alvin has tried to drag me into.

Do we even know him? How did he get caught up in something so dangerous that he's returned beaten and bloody? I lick my lips, my fear sending a jolt of pain through my chest.

Alvin's eyes dart to Josephine before she slips into the chair next to him and takes over unwrapping his hand. His body tenses as he watches her intently, wincing when the fabric pulls on his skin.

She's not going to push back at him. She'll do whatever he asks, even if it means picking her husband over her daughter. This—her theatrics—was all for show. When it comes to the men in her life, she'll always put them first because they can give her something I can't; *a different kind of companionship.* I've never known anything different in my twenty-two years of life, and I don't expect that to change now.

Alvin replies, unable to meet my eyes. "His name is Massimo Marino. He, uh, he owns a club in the city."

A laugh escapes me before I can stop it. It sounds harsh, bitter, and foreign to my ears. *I know that name.* "No." I straighten, ready to stand my ground.

What fresh hell of a universe have I walked into? This isn't normal, at least not in my world. Did he honestly think that I would be fine with marrying someone I don't know? I scoff, moving toward the counter and flattening my palms on the cool marble before I force myself to face them again.

Josephine's gentle sobs turn into wails worthy of an Oscar. My stomach churns when my attention drops to Alvin's mangled hand. He holds it up, blood dripping from where his pinkie finger should be. The raw stump is a stark display of the brutality he's forcing me into. I've heard of Massimo Marino and the reputation he has; I just never thought I'd see it firsthand.

I swallow down the bile that rises in my throat at the thought of being married to a monster like him. Someone who has no regard for the life of others. *There's no way I'm doing that.*

"If you don't do this, Margot, I'll be facing a lot worse than a missing finger," Alvin snaps, looking pointedly at his hand.

Nausea assails me, not because of the guilt Alvin's clearly trying to ambush me with, but because of the turmoil swirling in my gut. I don't want him being hurt, or worse, killed on my conscience, but I also will not be marrying a man I do not know.

"There has to be something else you can give him," I rush.

When he looks away sheepishly, I narrow my eyes, the pieces of the puzzle falling into place. "What exactly do you owe him?"

Alvin winces as Josephine tends to his hand, washing away his blood and inspecting the damage. "Money. I owe him money."

I wait for him to elaborate, but when it's clear that's not going to happen, I shake my head, tears of anger brimming in my eyes. "So that's it then?" I ask, my voice trembling with barely contained fury. "You sell me off like a piece of furniture that you no longer want, and for what? A debt you brought on yourself?" Shaking my head, I square my shoulders, my voice rising. "I won't do it. I'm not your collateral. You need to figure a way out of this without me. Your inability to own your actions is not my problem, so don't even try and put your consequences onto me."

Josephine cries out, her sobs loud and grating in the otherwise quiet house, but I block her out, holding Alvin's gaze and refusing to back down. Her chair scrapes across the floor and she staggers toward me, falling to her knees at my feet. "Please, Margot. You have to save him," she begs.

I stare down at her, my stomach churning, but I can't summon the same tears. If I felt any sympathy or familial love toward this woman, it's gone. After years of dealing with her, this is the final straw. I want nothing to do with either of them. I'd rather be alone in this world than have them in my life. "What about me and what I want?" I stab myself in the chest with my finger.

Tear-filled eyes lift to mine, Josephine's voice barely audible when she pleads, "I can't lose him."

"My happiness means nothing? I have to pay for his crimes?" I grit, my jaw tightening. She's always thinking about what she wants, what she needs, and never about others. *Never about me.*

Her features are pinched. "I am begging you, Margot. If I lose Alvin, I don't know what I'll do."

Go on with your life? I hate that she's so dependent on him, and he knows it. The way she behaves disgusts me. If she's taught me anything, it's how not to be independent. *To be nothing like her.*

Someone has to be the adult in this family—and it's clearly not her or Alvin. It never has been. And yet, I feel the weight of her sobs pressing on my chest, her pleas clawing at my resolve. My head screams at me to fight, to say no, to leave them to clean up their own mess. But when I look at Alvin's mangled hand and see the tears streaking Josephine's face, I know I'm already trapped.

"Fine," I say, my voice stronger than I feel. "I'll think about it."

With a squeal of joy, she jumps to her feet, wrapping me in her arms before leaving me oddly bereft as she crosses the room to him. I can't quiet the niggling voice in the back of my head that tells me I've been played; that my own flesh and blood has used her limited acting skills to get what she wants.

I take one last look at them, at the mess they've made of our lives before heading for my bedroom. Each step feels heavier than the last, my mind reeling as I grasp for some way out of this. I won't marry this monster. I'll fight every step of the way. *This isn't over.*

Not yet.

Chapter 3

Massimo

There's something captivating about this time of the day. Before it really begins, and the world awakens to shatter the calm quiet. I prefer it like this. There's a solitude to the air that allows me to see everything all at once, even if I'm not truly alone, with my driver in the car.

It's peaceful now, and the sky is painted in shades of gray and black, the morning not quite having pulled itself from the shadows of the night. Puddles reflect the dim glow of the streetlights, and a breeze blows through the air, sending a chill across my exposed skin.

A crow is perched on a lamppost across the street, its black eyes locked on me, a stark reminder that my reputation is never far behind. Some call me 'The Crow' because of how I dress, and others call me it, because when I find something I want, I take it.

I sip on my espresso, leaning against the car, watching

as the bird takes flight. Shifting my attention back to the house in front of me, I stuff a hand into my pocket to ward off the chill.

The peace that is a rarity in my world is brought to an abrupt halt by a petite redhead. *Right on time.* Her hand trails the wall of the house as she moves quietly toward the front from the back, her focus shifting between her feet and the darkness behind her. There's a careful precision in every step she takes.

She's even more beautiful than the picture Alvin showed me, and my body warms as she gets closer. But what strikes me in the chest and sends my blood pounding through my veins in a chaotic and yet glorious rhythm is the fierceness rolling off her in waves. It's followed by a wildness on its heels that has me questioning my decision to wipe Alvin's debt in exchange for her. I dismiss the thought almost immediately.

She will be a dutiful wife, whether she likes it or not. And if she doesn't fulfill her purpose, then she will no longer be of use to me. This marriage is only going ahead to get the men from the other families in New York off my back. They're adamant that I am too young and inexperienced when it comes to life to lead my family and have all, but said if I get married, they will respect me. Normally, I'd just take them out to silence their complaints, but we have too much going on for me to start more wars.

When Margot reaches the front of the house, she adjusts the duffel bag on her shoulder, pulling it higher. I watch, fascinated, as she huffs out a breath and winces when her long straight red hair gets caught in the strap.

It's only when she's freed herself and continues along the sidewalk that I push away from the car. "Going somewhere?" I call, my voice cutting through the quiet morning.

My eyes travel the length of her body, lingering on the curves outlined by her fitted long-sleeve top and leggings. I catch the way she stiffens at my words before forcing herself to relax. The action confirms what I already knew: my unwilling *fiancée* was planning an escape that I just foiled. I roll my lips together to keep my smile at bay. There's nothing I love more than outsmarting someone.

"Mr. Marino." She inclines her head, brazen disgust shining brightly in her gaze.

After a beat, she moves to stride past me, but I catch her elbow, forcing her to stop. For a moment, she struggles as she tries without success to free herself. I tighten my grip, waiting for her to look at me. When she finally does, I see the defiance shining bright in the depths of her green eyes, and my cock springs to life at the sight.

"Margot," I say, my voice deceptively soft. Her lips part, and when she inhales shakily, the corner of my mouth twitches. "I asked you a question."

Blinking, she drops her gaze to the hold I have on her arm and tugs again. I keep my hold firm, a muscle ticking in my jaw at her rebellion. Her fire meets my ice in an unspoken challenge when she returns her focus to me. "If this is how you plan on treating me, Mr. Marino..." She sneers my name, her petite nose wrinkling in disgust and rippling the freckles dusted across it. "Then you had better prepare for the war I will bring down on you."

Baring my teeth in a wolfish grin, I yank her toward me. Her eyes widen in shock and she lifts her hand, pressing it into my chest to keep her body from making full contact with my own. It's probably for the best, given the fact that I'm rock hard at this *tête-à-tête* we have going on.

I press my forehead into hers until I see a familiar emotion: pain. "Sweetheart, you clearly don't know who you're dealing with. But trust me when I say—you don't want to find out." Releasing her arm, I step back and pull on the sleeves of my black shirt as I look around the street. "Get in the car, Margot." There's no mistaking the warning in my tone.

She looks away, her eyes going glassy before she blinks them clear. A transformation overtakes her. It's evident in the hardening of her jaw and the narrowing of her eyes. She folds her arms over her chest and asks, "And if I don't?"

I take a step forward, invading her space and ignoring the fact that a thrill races through me at her challenge. *I'm going to have so much fun with her.* My voice is just a murmur, but the threat of what is to come is as clear as day. "Then you'll get a taste of exactly how our marriage will work. Your every step, every breath, every thought will be done by. My. Side."

I see something akin to fear flicker in her eyes before she shuts it down and stands taller. She tilts her head, releasing a laugh, but there's a hollowness to it. "Let me guess. You're used to women falling in line because you snap your fingers?" She emphasizes her point by snapping her fingers. "Well, I'm sorry to disappoint you, but I'm not like that. There isn't a world in which I bend to your will and—"

Her words are cut off when I take her bag and walk to the car. "Hey, where are you going with my stuff?" Indignation laces her words as she follows me.

I throw it in the backseat, and when I turn to face her, she takes a step back. "Get. In. Now."

"No." Her hands ball into fists at her side.

My fingers flex on the door and my nostrils flare. Fuck me, she's going to be a pain in my ass. "Wrong answer," I growl, grabbing her arm again.

She digs her heels in, but I'm stronger, and within a matter of seconds, I have her in front of the open car door. Her attention shifts to the bag on the far side of the backseat before returning to me. "Where are we going?" she asks, trying to hide the hint of fear in her tone.

Hearing her afraid doesn't make me feel alive in the way it usually does. But I don't dwell on it, refocusing myself on the whole purpose of my visit instead.

"I'm taking you wherever it is you are going to meet your *boyfriend*." My lip curls on the word. "You're going to tell him it's over and then you're going to prepare for your future, as my *wife*."

Margot's eyes widen, her breath coming in short, sharp gasps before she looks away, fiddling with the sleeve of her sweater. "I wasn't meeting anybody. I was going for a walk."

Liar.

"With a bag full of your things and looking over your shoulder like the hounds of hell are hot on your heels?" I raise a brow in question, amused at her attempt to convince me otherwise.

"My life is none of your business. Whatever deal you made with Alvin, that's for you to take up with him. Don't think for a second that you own me because my stepfather can't handle his debts. I am not for sale," she snaps. The strength in her tone is admirable, but the fact that she can't look me in the eye when she's talking is a giveaway about the doubt she has in what she's saying.

I reach out, gripping her chin and forcing her to look at me. This close, I can see the gold flecks in her eyes, the fire sparking in the depths. I could claim her, force her to submit, to forget the anger that she so desperately clings to. *No. That can wait.* The time will come for her to be on her knees, obeying my every command.

"That is where you are wrong, Margot. From the second you were offered to me, you became *mine*," I growl, my frustration building. Releasing her, I inhale, the faint hint of strawberries assailing my nostrils. Cracking my neck, I add, "The sooner you realize that, the better."

We stare at each other for a beat, her fire still burning

bright, before she rolls her eyes and climbs into the car. I half expect her to climb out of the other side; it's why I put the child lock on, but I'm pleasantly surprised when she sits back, pulling her bag into her lap.

Climbing in after her, I close the door behind me and engulf us in silence. Margot stares out the window, refusing to look at me, her bag in her lap and clutched tightly in her hands. In the reflection of the glass, I can see her taut features and practically hear the cogs turning in her mind. Based on our limited interaction, I'm guessing she's either trying to plot her escape or figuring out how badly she can hurt me before I can pull my gun out.

"Where to?" I ask out of courtesy rather than necessity because I know exactly where she's going. *That's why I'm here.*

She turns toward me, her eyes narrowed and sarcasm dripping from her every word when she retorts, "I'm sure you already know that."

I chuckle, the sound dark and sinister as it bounces around the confines of the car. Her eyes dart to Renato, my driver, before finding me. Leaning forward, I instruct, "To the abandoned warehouses by Sunset Industrial Park in Brooklyn."

Nodding, Renato puts the car in gear and navigates down the street, heading for the highway. A charged quiet falls over us; the only sounds are that of the city outside the car. Neither one of us is willing to speak first and so when Margot sighs heavily from her position beside me, I pull out my phone, checking my emails.

As we near the industrial park, I put my phone away. "Our wedding will be taking place by the end of next week. Break it off with him, Margot, or you won't like what will happen next."

She inhales sharply, her obvious torment cloaking us as she pleads, "Why? Why are you doing this? Why *me*?"

I run my tongue over my teeth, my gaze flicking over her from head to toe. "It makes sense business-wise."

She scoffs, returning her attention to the passing scenery. "Right, because that's a *normal* reason to marry a complete stranger."

"It is in my world..." I pause, waiting for her to look at me. "There's one thing I can promise you, Margot. I will keep you safe, but for me to do that, you need to learn the ways of the circles I keep, and that starts with you ending things with him."

"You can't make me," she bites, folding her arms over her chest in defiance, pushing her breasts up and together. My dick twitches in response and I grind my molars, frustrated with my body's natural reaction.

Shaking my head, I exhale heavily before reaching out for her. My hand slips around her throat like it belongs there, my tattooed flesh a contrast to her perfection. Applying a light pressure, I warn, "Defy me, Margot, and I'll make sure he doesn't live to see another day. And if you think I'm bluffing, try me and see what happens, but I guarantee you won't like it."

Renato pulls the car to a stop at the entrance of the industrial park, leaving the engine to idle. I see the war she's fighting inside of herself. She's questioning if she should take the risk or submit to the inevitable.

Her hand lifts to open the door, but she stops when I say, "I'll be waiting here, ready to make my move if you're not back in fifteen minutes."

Margot steps from the car, the weight of my threat hanging in the air between us before she slams the door closed. I lean back, watching her retreating figure and the gentle sway of her hips. I'll have no problem making good on my promise if she's not back here in fifteen minutes.

I draw my gun from the holster at my waist, ejecting the magazine to check the rounds before returning it and racking. Resting it on my knee, I stare out of the window in the direction she walked.

Chapter 4

Margot

A breeze howls through the buildings, rattling the loose window panes. Ethan pulls me into his body, his warmth a comfort I've come to know and love over the last five years. Closing my eyes, I drag his citrusy scent deep into my lungs, hating how I compare it to Massimo's woodsy musk.

Squeezing him closer, I exhale, wishing that we could stay here for the rest of our lives. The threat Massimo made in the car hangs heavily over my head like a guillotine, and although I want nothing more than to run away with Ethan, I can't have his life being taken because of me.

I can't hide the pleading note when I ask, "Promise me something?"

"For you? I'd do anything, Margot. You know that," Ethan murmurs, his nose stroking the column of my neck as he squeezes me tighter for half a second.

I tip my head back, giving him better access. It's easier to sink into the pleasure that dissipates the tension when he's doing that. In hindsight, it probably wasn't a good idea to meet here; a place we've fooled around in countless times. *Our place.* Not when I'm delivering the news I have to. But then again, I thought I was coming here to convince him to run away with me.

The reminder of our circumstance is like ice water thrown on the flames of my arousal, and I suck in a lungful of air. Tears well in my eyes and a sharp pain makes itself known in the back of my throat. *I don't want to do this.* I don't want us to *end,* but I have no choice. I won't have Ethan's blood on my hands; I won't have anybody's blood on my hands. And that's the problem, no matter what I do, somebody will die and I'll have to live with that. The only way to stop that from happening is to sacrifice myself and *marry* Massimo. He's made that abundantly clear.

Leaning away from him, I tuck back the rogue curl that hangs over his forehead, my eyes remaining locked on the patch of skin visible at the base of his throat. A thickness threatens to choke me as I push out the words I have no choice but to voice. "Promise me you'll remember how you feel about me right now. That you'll remember you *loved* me."

Ethan's hands move to hold my arms, forcing me back as he dips his gaze to search my face, his confusion evident. "What are you talking about?"

He's usually so good at reading me, but right now, I

need him to make me this promise, no questions asked. If he doesn't, I don't know that I'll have the strength to speak the words I need to. Words that will stick with me for the rest of my life. *Words that will save him.* My eyes blur as I tear my gaze away from his.

His grip tightens, shaking me lightly. Panic sends his voice an octave higher when he says, "M? You're scaring me. What's going on?"

A tear slips free, followed by another, and I take comfort in his presence one final time because I know once I say what I need to, he won't be offering me comfort. He'll hate me.

Burying my face in his chest, I cry out, "Please, Ethan. Just say that you promise you'll remember?"

"Okay. Okay." He wraps his arms around me, talking into my hair. "Okay... I promise. I won't ever stop loving you. I'll never forget the love I *feel* for you. You're it for me, Margot."

The tin walls rattle as a gust of wind slams into the building, reminding me of the desolate location we're in and the time limit on the task I'm still yet to complete.

Pushing out of his embrace, I swipe angrily at the tears that won't stop. *I shouldn't have to do this.* It shouldn't be me having to give up the person I've loved for the last five years. He's my first love and I know he'll be my *only* love. We had plans for a future together and I can feel it being ripped from my grasp with every second that passes.

Anger swirls at my helplessness, igniting the edges

like a burning sheet of paper. I hate that Josephine, Alvin, and Massimo get to dictate my life, that they can yank away my future with deadly threats.

Ethan Watkins has been my best friend since we were both in diapers. Even our moms were best friends. When Josephine married Alvin, I was fifteen, and he moved us away, out of the city and too far away from Ethan for us to see each other. We kept in touch, and when we turned seventeen, he showed up on my front porch and asked me out. For the last five years, he's shown me what true love is, and every day of my life has been like a movie.

Up until last night.

Folding my arms across my stomach, I gaze over his shoulder. It's an effort to get the words past my lips. "I... I can't..." I clear my throat and nod decisively before meeting his confused yet patient gaze. "I can't do this anymore, Ethan. I wish I could, but I can't."

"What?" His mouth lifts, a chuckle falling from his lips as he shakes his head. "Very funny, M."

He reaches for me, but I take a step back, numbness creeping into my body. It's for the best that I don't feel a thing. I'll go into this marriage to Massimo with my heart closed off and burning with the flames of my hatred.

"I'm sorry." My voice is barely above a whisper. "But I'm breaking up with you, Ethan."

I need him to believe me.

He runs his fingers through his thick chestnut brown hair and begins pacing the cracked concrete. I watch, mesmerized, as the weeds that have grown through are trampled beneath his feet. Turning toward me, with wide, glassy eyes, he pleads, "You don't mean that, M."

"I do mean it." I bite down on the side of my cheek, swallowing thickly.

Ethan tips his head back before returning his gaze to me. I see the anger and confusion warring inside of him before he snaps, "No, you're not...You're... you're messing with me. You just made me fucking promise to remember that I loved you and now you're playing some sort of sick, twisted game. It's not funny, Margot." His words echo around us, a bite of frustration laced with panic in his tone.

I lift my chin, resting my hand on my chest to ease the tightness taking up residence. *This isn't fair*. None of this is. I don't have a choice but to hurt the one person that's always been on my side. Either he dies and becomes another casualty of my stepfather's mess, or I make him hate me, but he gets to live a long, fruitful life.

It's a no-brainer.

"I'm being serious, Ethan. I can't be with you. I don't want this." I wave a finger between us. "Anymore." The conviction in my tone is surprising. This is far from what I want, but if I want him to live, I have to do this. His eyes brim with unshed tears and the hurt that falls over his expression before he turns away nearly kills me.

His voice is small and there's a hint of resignation in his tone when he asks, "Why are you doing this?" He doesn't even look back at me; as if it hurts him too much to see me again.

"I..." I can't tell him the real reason, but I don't want to lie any more than I have to. My heart is breaking too. I suck in a breath before looking at his stiff back. "I'm getting married." *That's the truth.* "And I love him, Ethan." *That's a lie.*

A gasp of shock leaves him. I want to reach out, pull him close, and tell him the truth, but then he'd try to fix this and there isn't anything either of us can do. Especially if what I know about Massimo Marino is true, and given the threat he made in the car, I know that it is.

Ethan walks away without a glance in my direction, out of the warehouse, out of danger, and out of my life. I hate every second of watching him leave. This moment will stay with me forever, etching itself into my heart like an ugly scar. I'll never forgive Josephine for what she has asked of me, and I'll spend the rest of my life making sure Massimo pays for making me do this.

But at least Ethan will be alive.

Even if I'll never have the life I wanted.

Chapter 5

Massimo

The faint creak from the doorway pulls my attention from the report I'm reviewing. I don't need to look up to know it's Daniele—the exhaustion rolling off him mirrors my own. We've been working tirelessly, chasing shadows, trying to flush out the people who dared to attack my family. It's a hunt we won't stop until their spilled blood is on our hands.

Mattia—Aurora's uncle—confirmed that we have a rat, somewhere in our ranks, before Aurora shot him in the head for kidnapping her. He thought, under the poor advice of someone in *my* house, that Romeo would give up everything for Aurora. Maybe he would have, but for a moment, he thought she was the one conspiring against us.

The reminder brings to the surface a thought that I haven't been able to shake since we got Aurora back. Why frame her if they wanted to use her as bait? Unless that was their play all along. Cut Mattia out—use him to do their dirty work and it doesn't matter if he dies in the process.

Well, it didn't work. We will find them and force them to face the consequences of trying to go against us. *I won't stop until they're dead.*

Daniele moves further into the room and I look up from the folder in front of me, welcoming the break. The pile I've been assessing has grown over the past couple of hours, with my men having passed through to deliver updates on various aspects of my operations. Numbers tumble through my mind from the financial report, but I blink them away and ask, "What have you got?"

As well as searching for the woman, Anastasia, who tortured Aurora when she was being held captive, Daniele is also searching for Elio Moretti. We've been informed by some reliable sources that he has been the one funding the operation to take us down.

Falling onto the couch at the back of the room, Daniele runs a hand down his face and rests his head on the back cushions. "Nothing?" He huffs out a cynical laugh. "We're no further to finding out who the rat is. Elio is deeper underground than anyone is willing to share, and as you know, there hasn't been any more activity since Mattia was killed. And given our inability to question him before." He pauses, raising a pointed brow and leaving me to fill in the rest. "We don't have any leads to find them. Callum has been monitoring the phones, but again, there's been nothing. Not a single call has been made from any of the landlines." His vexation is clear in the bite to his words.

Callum 'used to' work for the Irish mafia, but after his father was murdered, he stepped away, moving off the grid and doing odd IT jobs here and there. He's been instrumental in helping us in our search for the people behind the attacks. More recently, he's been looking into our phone records after it appeared Haven—the house-keeper Leonardo is tracking down—took a phone call from a number connected to the Russians.

I stand, crossing the room, and taking a seat opposite Daniele in one of the armchairs. Tapping my fingers on the armrest, I exhale heavily. "If we've exhausted every avenue, dig deeper. Question everyone—no exceptions. Tell Callum to tap the cellphones of anyone that so much as steps foot on the property. I don't care how invasive it gets; whatever we need to do to find these bastards, we do it. There isn't a reality in which they get away with this."

Even as I issue the order to Daniele, frustration gnaws at me. We've been at this for weeks and we're no closer than we were at the start. The anger burns in my chest, but I shove it down, refusing to allow it to engulf me. I'll only make mistakes if I do. Our every move has to be calculated and measured, at least until we find them and then I'll make them wish they'd never crossed me.

Daniele nods, his jaw tightening as he sits forward and rests his elbows on his knees. *"Capisco."* We fall quiet for a moment, the faint hum of the air conditioning the only sound before Daniele asks, "Will Leonardo be returning soon? I could use his help with the meetings, given his knowledge of the men."

Scrubbing a hand over my chin, I lean back into my chair, crossing my leg over my knee. "No. The situation with tracking down Haven is..." I pause, searching for the right words. "Proving more difficult than first thought. I've told him not to return until he's found her."

Daniele nods. "I assume you've updated Romeo about the extension of my stay?"

Cracking my neck, I reply, "He's going to be visiting soon for my wedding. Whilst he's here, we can discuss bringing another person into the fold and strategize on how we can bring this situation to a close, sooner rather than later."

Keeping his features neutral, Daniele leans forward, holding his hand out to me. "Congratulations, Massimo. I didn't know you were seeing anyone."

I huff out a laugh. The irony is not lost on me that Romeo said the exact same thing when I called him with the news. "Thank you. It's... *very* new."

"Well, I can't wait to meet your bride. She must be quite something to have captured your attention."

She sure is. Clearing my throat, I reply, "Let's get back to business. What do you have on the ever elusive Anastasia?"

Daniele chuckles, relaxing back into his seat. "Now, this is an interesting one. I've asked around about her with some of the connections Leonardo gave me. She was born in Russia, daughter of a carpenter and baker. Those are the only facts I could gather. She's a ghost, but with a lot of folklore following her around.

"According to the stories I've been told, when she was twelve, her parents sent her and her brother to the US to live with an aunt and uncle. I think the expectation was that she would get an education and build a life for herself, but instead, they were trafficked. There's no doubt about it, she was groomed into what she is today."

"A 'fixer' of sorts," I reply, cracking my knuckles.

"That's one thing to call her. She's been hired to take out some of the biggest players in our world. Her ability to disappear into the shadows is what makes her lethal. She slips past even the most vigilant of security. We're lucky we were able to get a description of her from Aurora. Others who have seen her face haven't lived to describe it." Daniele pauses, his gaze on the trees swaying under the weight of the storm that's gathering beyond the rain-splattered window. When he returns his attention to me, he says, "It looks like her brother was in the warehouse where they were holding Aurora. I wouldn't be surprised if we're on her shit list, considering none of their men made it out alive when we attacked it."

Which means she'll be out there plotting her revenge, and I can add another thing to consider to my already overflowing plate. "Find her," I reply, my voice a low growl. "And kill her before she convinces someone else it's worth it to fuck with us."

"I'm on it." Daniele stands, heading for the door. When he reaches it, he asks, "Do you want me to bring her back here when I find her?" Something flickers in his gaze. Conflict? Doubt? It doesn't matter. He'll do what needs to be done, for the family. *For Aurora.* They have a unique bond, given the fact that he was the only one who didn't think she'd betrayed us. If he hadn't gone digging, she'd have died in that warehouse with none of us knowing the truth.

Rubbing my thumb along the line of my jaw, I reply, "No. Just kill her."

"Got it." He jerks his head in confirmation.

When the door clicks shut, I tip my head back, staring at the ceiling. The weight of the betrayal from a man in my own ranks has been sitting on my chest like a lead weight since the warehouse. It's suffocating, relentless, and a constant reminder that someone I've put my trust in has sold us out. A weaker man would have broken by now, but weakness isn't a luxury I'm afforded. *Not now. Not ever.*

My focus has to be on finding the rat. They were adamant on getting us out of New York; a drive like that doesn't just disappear, it festers, waiting for the perfect moment to strike again. They'll be out there, regrouping, planning their next move, but we'll find them and when we do, they'll wish they'd never taken us on.

Chapter 6

Margot

Standing in the middle of the changing room, I barely recognize the woman staring back at me. She's a stranger dressed in white, suffocating in layers of tulle and lies.

My chest tightens, and for a fleeting moment, I wonder if I could survive in prison. If I set this place on fire and got caught, could I make it? Would I even be sent to prison for a first offense? Yeah, I think they take arson quite seriously, so that has to be a yes, regardless of whether it's my first time or not.

Refocusing my mind, I run my hands over the white, puffy, and yet somehow also scratchy material of the wedding gown Josephine picked out for me. We've been in Bridal Bells—the *third* bridal store in as many days—for three excruciating hours.

I have a headache, which isn't helped by the bright

overhead light reflecting off the pristine mirror and the clogging, sickly sweet scent of roses and champagne that hangs in the air. Josephine has been driving me crazy, pushing me into dress after dress, and acting like I might actually *want* to marry Massimo.

A package was delivered a few days after we'd officially met. It set out the details of our wedding, where it would take place, how many guests were coming, and where I could find a gown. That was the last I heard from Massimo and I haven't seen him since he dropped me back after I broke things off with Ethan.

Ethan.

My chest constricts and my breaths turn shallow at the thought of my childhood sweetheart. His reaction when I told him I was going to marry someone else has haunted me. My heart shattered that day and now I'm drifting through life, my anger burning hot and heavy in my chest, with no hope of ever healing.

A knock on the door draws my attention away from my sullen thoughts and everything comes back into stark clarity, as if a bucket of ice water has been thrown over me. Staring at my reflection, I pull in a deep breath, wincing when the confines of the corset boning dig into my ribs. Annoyance adds a bite to my tone when I call, "What do you want?"

I know it'll be Josephine. She's hovered in every store, like she's worried I'll make a run for it. Truth be told, I would. Hell, I tried to the morning I met Massimo, and look how well that went. But unfortunately for me, there are no windows in this goddamn place. Not that it would make much difference, I'm sure Massimo will have his men watching the building, just like he's had them watching me since we met.

"Margot, darling?" Josephine calls her voice a mix of tense excitement and exasperation. "Are you coming out? The assistant said this one might just be *the one*."

Yeah. It might be the one that makes me snap. I roll my eyes, adjusting the neckline and wishing I was anywhere but here. Gathering up the skirt, I unlock the door and yank it open, causing Josephine to jump out of my path. I stride out of the room, refusing to look at her. Instead, I keep my focus on the mirror and the podium in front of it.

Josephine gasps, her voice soft and breathless when I step onto it to showcase the monstrosity I'm wearing. "Oh, *mon chéri*, you look so beautiful."

I close my eyes, the pain of everything I've lost mixing with my rage and swirling like a tornado inside of me. A heavy sigh escapes me and I harden my jaw, before opening my eyes. No good will come from giving into the emotions. My future has already been determined and I have no choice if I want to keep Ethan alive. Massimo made that abundantly clear.

My attention shifts to Josephine, her face coated in joy and her hands clasped in front of her chest. Delight makes her gray eyes shine brighter than they should, given the sacrifice I'm making. *I hate her*. We haven't always gotten along, but I never thought I'd have such a strong emotion toward her.

"Can you give us a moment?" I ask the two assistants fluttering around me as they adjust the dress and try their hardest to make a sale.

"Of course, we'll be right outside if you need anything or want to try on a different dress." The store owner smiles before following the other woman out.

Stepping down from the podium, I walk toward the chairs and take a seat, my focus on not ripping a dress I have no intention of ever wearing again. Josephine hovers in my periphery, her happiness morphing into anxiousness and rippling through me with a suffocating intensity. "What's wrong, *mon chéri?*"

I bite down on the inside of my cheek. She only calls me that when she wants something and I hate that, along with everything she touches, she's managed to turn the term of endearment into something ugly and tarnished.

At my silence, she continues, her worry evident in the slight hitch in her tone, "You promised you would do this, Margot. You know what's on the line."

She's right. I know exactly what's at stake: my freedom and being with the man I love. The man that no longer wants anything to do with me. "I don't know if I can do this. I don't know if I can marry a man I don't know, one that could have me killed without a second thought. And the fact that you're okay with me going

44

through with this..." My words trail off, unable to find the right ones to express myself.

Josephine falls into the seat next to me, reaching for my hand and staring at me with tear-brimmed eyes. "No, no, no, no. You have to do this, Margot. I can't lose Alvin, and besides, Massimo will provide you with a good life. He will. He's got money and—"

I cut her off, standing from my seat and pulling out of her hold. My anger spills over and fills the room with a darkness that neither of us can hide from. "Do you really think that matters to me? I'm nothing like you," I spit, my venom sending Josephine's head rearing back. "Massimo Marino could have all the money in the world and it wouldn't change a damn thing. You have made me give up the love of *my* life so that you can keep a man that is willing to trade your child in payment for his own mistakes. Let that sink in and then come and talk to me about what you can and can't lose."

Shaking my head, I grab fistfuls of tulle and storm to the changing room, ignoring her soft weeping. It's probably her attempt at making me feel bad, at guilting me into doing what she wants me to do. The thought infuriates me and when I enter the room, I slam the door behind me; the force shaking the walls.

A sob rises from my chest, tightening the muscles to an almost unbearable ache. I struggle to inhale, fumbling with the lock on the door before sliding to the floor and letting my tears tumble down my cheeks unchecked.

Why is everything so out of my control?

No, I refuse to think like that, as if everything is slipping through my fingers.

I am strong.

I am brave.

I can face this marriage with my chin held high and make Massimo's life hell.

Can't I?

Yes, goddamn it.

My phone vibrates on the bench with a message and I swipe angrily at my cheeks before reaching for it. Hope that it might be Ethan flutters in my chest, but it's soon snuffed out when I read the name of my girlfriend, Reagan.

I wish I didn't have to lie to Ethan about why I did what I did. More than anything, I wish we had a future that wasn't dictated by the actions of my stepfather and the selfishness of my mother. In reality, I don't know that Ethan will ever forgive me, but I do know that I won't stop trying to make it right between us. Maybe one day I can tell him the truth.

Wiping the wetness from underneath my chin, I pull up the text conversation with Ethan.

MARGOT

I'm so sorry, Ethan.

I love you.

ETHAN

I'm tired of all your apologies, Margot. Besides, if you really loved me, you wouldn't have broken up with me.

MARGOT

I know.

ETHAN

Is that all I'm going to get? An 'I know'?
After five years?

MARGOT

I can't give you any more than that. You
deserve it, but I can't.

ETHAN

Are you safe?

MARGOT

I am, but there are bigger things at play
that I have no control over.

It's been two days since I sent that message and he's not responded. We used to talk every day and now all I have left are my memories and the chain of messages that ended abruptly. My fingers fly across the screen, typing out a message that I don't know he'll ever read.

MARGOT

I don't deserve your forgiveness or your
support, but you're the only one who
really knows me. My wedding is on
Saturday, at St. Bart's on Park Avenue.
The ceremony starts at 12 noon. I really
would like you to come.

Chewing on my bottom lip, I hover my thumb over the send button before pressing it. The screen confirms the message has been delivered, but the silence that follows feels loud and brash. My heart feels heavy and on the verge of breaking all over again.

I know that I'm being selfish, wanting him to be there as a comforting presence, to give me something to hold on to from my lost future. And yet, I can't help but wonder, will he come? Or have I broken him as much as I have myself?

Chapter 7

Margot

I t's my wedding day.

    I should be happy and excited for a future with my husband, but all I feel is dread that sits heavy in the pit of my stomach. The black dress I've chosen says it all—this isn't a celebration. It's a funeral of my freedom. A light drizzle taps a steady beat against the stained-glass windows as if the sky itself mourns for me.

We've been at the church since eight this morning and only now am I finally alone. I've had to put on a show, smiling and gushing to everyone that wished me well.

If only they knew.

The lead up to today has shown me just how good of an actress I am. It seems Josephine passed something on to me, aside from her looks. I've been paraded around town like a prize pig, meeting people who never would have known I existed had I not been exchanged for Alvin's debt.

Moving to stand in front of the full length, gold-framed mirror, I take in my reflection and the haunted woman staring back at me. I always thought I'd get married in a white dress; something timeless and representative of the romantic air that a wedding day should be filled with. But the one I've chosen for today—a day of mourning—is more fitting.

With a daring halter neckline that wraps around my neck and leaves my shoulders and collarbone bare, it does exactly what I need it to do—showcase my spirit and rebellion to this marriage. My favorite part about it—and the part that I'm hoping will piss my soon-to-be-husband off—is the deep V-cut that plunges down the center of my chest from the base of my throat to the waistband of the skirt.

Josephine will have a conniption over the 'disrespect' of my dress choice. But I couldn't care less. After our run-in at the bridal store, I told her I didn't want her help with picking out a dress or any input from her with the wedding. She protested, but it wasn't exactly heartfelt because deep down, she only wants one thing: for me to go through with this marriage and save Alvin's sorry ass.

This entire situation is a farce.

And yet, it's my reality. The thought sends a tremor racing through my body. I swallow hard, thinking of Ethan and the future we've lost. I don't want to do this, but what's the alternative? I run away and Massimo finds me anyway? Yeah, and then he kills me, as well as Alvin. I might not like Alvin, but I'm not going to be the reason he's dead, because I know the threats Massimo has made aren't threats at all but guarantees.

I hate that I've been put in this situation, that I mean so little to Josephine that she's gone along with Alvin's plan. But most of all, I hate that I agreed to this.

Maybe, if I just do what Massimo asks of me, he'll grant me a divorce in a year or two and I can take back my life.

A laugh bubbles up, spilling from my lips and filling the room. There will be nothing for me once Massimo has put his ring on my finger. That much I know. I'll be stuck living a life that brings me no joy, with a man I have no hope of loving. And given his ruthless reputation, it's very possible that Massimo will force himself upon me. The thought has a knot of dread settling in the pit of my stomach.

Staring at the ceiling, I blink to ease the burning in the back of my eyes. I inhale through my nose, my senses assaulted by the slightly musky scent of the room. It's heavy and a reminder of where I am and all that is yet to come.

A hint of my strawberry shampoo clashes with the smell, reinforcing just how out of place I am in this church. I'm not a religious person and the fact that I'm going to recite vows that I don't mean, in the house of

God, makes me feel like a fraud. This wouldn't have been my choice of location. Nothing about this wedding—aside from my dress—has been my choice.

On an exhale, I roll back my shoulders and meet my gaze in the mirror. If this is going to be forced upon me, I'm going to make Massimo regret it. When I'm done with him, he'll regret ever thinking he could control me.

Even as the thought takes root, a sliver of doubt creeps in. *What if I can't?* What if his will to control me is stronger than my will to fight back? *No.* I refuse to think that will ever happen.

I don't think, I just act, diving my hands into my hair and pulling the pins holding it up out. The pain as strands are pulled from the roots doesn't faze me. It spurs me on, and I revel in the feeling.

My hair falls in disarray down my shoulders and I swipe up a hairbrush left behind by the hairstylist. Dragging it through my hair, I grit my teeth as it passes over each knot.

An idea quickly forms in my mind and I throw the hairbrush onto the table, my eyes scanning the contents. Triumphantly, I snatch up a tub of gel, unscrewing the cap and digging in three fingers. I hesitate for half a second, staring at my reflection before releasing a heavy exhale. *There's no going back once I do this.*

With a smile on my face, I lift my hand and smooth the gel through my hair until it's pushed back from my face, leaving me with a sleek yet wild look that screams defiance. It's perfect for a bride in black and makes my normally vibrant copper hair dark, like the color of dried blood.

For the first time since I was told of my fate, I feel alive. An energy thrums through me, part nerves, part excitement for the reaction I *know* Massimo will have. From the moment I met him, there was an air of control to him, like every aspect of his life is perfect and falls into place.

Well, not anymore.

Today, I vow to flip Massimo Marino's life upside down. After all, I have nothing to lose, and maybe if I push him far enough, he'll set me free. *Or kill me.* I suck in a shaky breath at the thought before forcing it from my mind.

Turning away from my reflection, I search the table littered with makeup products. *My subtle makeup won't do.* I need to make a statement with war paint because you should never go to battle ill-prepared.

Using a kohl eyeliner, I draw on a winged line before moving to my lower waterline and filling it in. When I'm satisfied, I throw the pencil on the table before searching for a lipstick that will do the dramatic eye makeup justice.

I can barely contain the grin that splits across my face when I uncap a black lipstick. What are the chances that a bridal makeup artist would have this? It must be my lucky day. I scoff before wiping it with my finger and dabbing it onto my lips. Using a clean finger to clean up the edges, I step back, admiring my reflection.

Perfect.

I feel elegant and sophisticated, but most importantly, I feel ready for the war that is yet to come.

A knock on the door pulls my attention from the woman in the mirror. I press my palm to my chest in an effort to ease the fluttering of nerves.

"It's time, Margot," Valentina, the wedding coordinator calls, her voice muffled as it travels through the heavy oak between us.

"Give them hell," I tell my reflection before picking up my flowers and marching toward the door. I hesitate for a second, my hand wrapped around the perfectly arranged bouquet of white roses. There's no going back, no escaping. Once I open this door, I'll be trapped in a circumstance I have no say in.

Blinking back my tears of anger, I inhale sharply, before pulling the door open. My lips twitch in amusement at the panic flaring in Alvin's eyes at the sight of me. *Good.* It's because of him that I'm in this mess. Valentina is quicker to cover her surprise. Instead, she clears her throat, waving her arm for me to go ahead.

I stride past them both, my head held high as I walk down the hallway to the narthex. Every step I take exposes my left leg through the thigh-high slit of the dress. There's something sinful about it. The sound of my heels on the tiled flooring echoes around the space and mixes with the soft swoosh of material as I move.

Behind me, Alvin follows the train of my dress, his movements hurried but hesitant. Josephine was insistent on me letting him walk me down the aisle. I agreed to save myself the argument, but I have no intention of letting that coward of a man give me away when he's the reason I'm in this situation.

When I reach the double doors that lead into the chapel, I come to a stop, urging the storm swirling inside of me to calm, at least for a moment. Alvin comes to a stop beside me, holding his arm out in preparation. I stare down at it, not bothering to hold back the curling of my lip.

Ignoring him, I push through the doors.

All eyes turn to me and I lift my chin high as I start my descent into hell. Alvin trails behind me like a bad smell that won't go away. I keep my gaze on my best friends, Cece and Reagan, as they stand at the front of the church. They're my allies in this, even if I haven't been able to bring myself to tell them the full story.

After half a beat, the wedding march begins, but I don't keep its pace as I march down the aisle. The chapel feels suffocating, with every eye in the room burning into me, their muttered words indistinct. I feel their stares on my skin, as intimate as a caress—curious, pitying, mocking. They don't know that this story doesn't end happily, but I can see the questions in their eyes. Their curiosity etched into their expressions as they wonder where I came from and how I've managed to find myself marrying a man like Massimo.

I'm no more than a quarter of the way toward the altar when, as if drawn on instinct, my gaze lands on Ethan. The sight of him, his face etched with sorrow, hits me like a punch to the gut.

The dull ache in my chest sharpens, stealing my breath and threatening to unravel me. For a moment, I forget where I am, consumed by the loss of him. The emotion that I've become so familiar with in the loneliness of night, wraps around my throat like a hand, choking me.

I drag my focus away, desperate to not show the imposing man that will soon be my husband any sign of weakness. When my gaze lands on Massimo, his eyes sweep over me, his jaw tightening before his gaze returns to my face. Something flashes in the depths—maybe amusement or annoyance—before a shutter comes down and his expression hardens.

I just want today to be over with.

———

"You may now kiss the bride."

That's it. I'm married. My eyes seek out Ethan, my anchor in the stormy sea that is now my life. I want to plead with him to forgive me, but it would be no use. His heartache mirrors my own, and I know no amount of begging or apologies will ever make this okay.

A hand snakes around my neck and my chin is turned back to Massimo. He's closer than I remember and there's a devilish darkness in his gaze that I can see projecting from his soul. Slowly, his mouth descends on mine at the same time as his hand tightens a fraction on my neck as he pulls me closer.

I don't have time to move or push him away and I don't fight him like I should. I'm too caught off guard at the fact that Massimo would do anything so intimate as *kiss his wife* to do anything.

The first brush of his lips over mine is strangely soft and testing. But then he captures my lips again, his kiss both commanding and far more possessive of me than he has any right to be. I feel like I'm drowning, with no hope of reaching the surface.

When he opens his mouth, mine follows suit and he takes the opportunity to dip his tongue between my lips. He tastes like toothpaste and something else that makes my body react in a wanton way.

I've never been kissed like this before.

There's an animalistic quality to it and, for a moment, I imagine what it would be like to experience Massimo in all of his glory.

He's intoxicating and although my body wants to sink into him, my head wins out. I fist my hands by my side as I come to my senses, disgusted with myself for entertaining the idea of wanting this monster. Especially when the man I love is feet away from me.

Massimo breaks the kiss, stepping back with a smug smirk on his face as he wipes away the remnants of my lipstick. He takes my hand before turning and stalking down the aisle, uncaring that I'm wearing five-inch heels and unprepared for how fast he's moving.

When we step out of the church, a barrage of paparazzi is waiting for us. Flashes from their cameras blind me and I hold up a hand to protect my eyes. Massimo drags me across the sidewalk to the waiting car, opening the door before maneuvering me between him and the vehicle. Without question, I slide in, breathing a sigh of relief when he closes the door and the indecipherable questions become muted.

The quiet is interrupted for a moment when Massimo climbs in beside me from the other side. He slams his door closed and instructs, "Back to the house, Renato."

The car moves forward at an agonizingly slow pace but as the church disappears from view, Massimo says, "That little display in the chapel, with the loving looks between you and your *ex*, was cute. But I hope you understand that will be the last time you see each other."

Running my tongue over my teeth, I bite back, "We'll see about that. Last I checked, you weren't my keeper and I'm not your prisoner."

Massimo removes his wedding ring, holding it between us as a strobe of light beams through the front windshield, reflecting off of the metal. "This makes you mine, Margot. And the promise I made to you the day we met still stands: I will not hesitate to kill him."

I roll my eyes and sigh as I stare at the passing landscape, ignoring the worry that gnaws in my gut. This is my life now—entirely out of my hands and with a man that I'm not sure is capable of feeling *anything*. I watch in the reflection of the glass as Massimo slips his wedding band into his pocket, vowing to myself that I won't let him take any more from me than he already has.

Chapter 8

Massimo

E xhaustion tugs at me, making every step feel heavier than the last as I head for my bedroom. No. *Our bedroom*. It's going to take a while to get used to thinking like that. I'm married, tethered to a woman who despises me.

We held an intimate reception at the house after the ceremony this afternoon. I left Margot to deal with the guests, excusing myself to my office with Romeo, Daniele, and Leonardo. Who would have thought that my wedding night would have been filled with talks about guns and drugs rather than getting lost in the body of *my wife?*

Fuck.

I'm married.

If I'm being honest with myself, I don't know what that entails in its entirety. We've said vows and promised each other till death do us part—although I wouldn't have put it past Margot to be plotting that already—but what does it mean for my everyday life? I'll share my bed with her. But will she bear my children?

I can't help but chuckle at the thought. If her dress choice is anything to go by, Margot has no plans to submit and fulfill the role of my dutiful wife. And I'm not the sort of man that will force himself upon a woman if she's not into it. I walk away. But there's something about the way she fights me at every turn that thrills me and makes my dick hard. It's safe to say that married life will be interesting with her, if nothing else.

I turn the corner and walk the dark corridor. When I open the door to our room, I'm greeted by an emptiness in the air. Only the lingering scent of her perfume, mingling with my scent is left to taunt me.

Margot fucking Marino.

Grinding my teeth, I flick on the overhead light, my eyes on the empty California king bed. *I should have seen this coming.* A quick search of the bathroom and closet confirms what I already know to be true. *She's gone.* The question is, has she left the house or just found another room?

Pulling my phone from my pocket, I scan through my messages and emails but there's nothing from the guys manning the security room or anything about a runaway bride. Okay. She'll have hidden herself in another room, probably the one furthest from me.

My strides are purposeful, my exhaustion gone and replaced with a primal determination to show Margot *exactly* who is in charge. I prowl through the dark corridors, the eerie quiet following me as I skulk through the house. Occasionally, the faint hum of the air conditioning or a creaky floorboard as I move breaks up the silence.

There aren't many rooms she could have gone to; most are off-limits and locked or not fit for guests to sleep in, either lacking furniture or with it covered. I move through the house with cold, deliberate precision, bypassing rooms and heading for the ones furthest away from ours.

The irritation in my chest swells, growing hotter and hotter. But there's something else, a constant that lingers beneath the surface. A hunger that I can't ignore. I've had men piss themselves at the sight of me, but Margot... she's like nobody I've ever met before. She doesn't fear me the way she should.

Rushing up a flight of stairs, I mutter, "If she wants to play games." My eyes are locked on the door at the end of the hallway. "Then let's fucking play." I roll my shoulders back, lifting my chin as I bare my teeth.

Fury guides me through the door. It slams against the wall, bouncing back toward me before I bring my palm against it to stop it from coming back at me. If she wanted to keep me out, she should have fucking locked it.

But even that wouldn't have been enough.

My nostrils flare as my eyes acclimate to the darkness of the room. Light spills in from behind me, but I can see her easily enough, curled up in bed, unmoving. I prowl across the room, my body vibrating with anger and my eyes set on her.

As I get closer, she sighs heavily, rolling onto her back and leaning up on her elbows. "What do you want? I'm trying to sleep."

I don't say a word. Instead, I continue my advance toward her until I reach the end of the bed where I throw back the covers. My jaw works at the sight before me. Margot's long legs are bare, smooth and begging to be touched. She pulls down *my T-shirt* in an attempt to cover herself and my dick hardens.

"What are you doing, Massimo?" There's a breathless note to her voice, but I can't be certain that I'm not imagining it.

Either way, my cock twitches, and an idea forms in my mind. I grip her ankle and drag her toward me. Margot yelps, her eyes widening and panic flaring in the emerald depths as she tries to stop herself from moving.

With her hair splayed out on the bed, the natural copper is a stark contrast to the white of the sheets beneath her. If it wasn't for the shock that's now morphed into a scowl, I might think she was alluring.

My voice is a cocktail of arousal and barely contained ire when I say, "You want to act out, Margot? See how far you can push me?" Defiance burns in her gaze. "Then bring it on, because you play stupid games, you win stupid prizes, and I know you won't fucking like how this turns out for you."

I reach for her, fisting the material of my T-shirt as I

pull her up, slow and deliberate. Her body stiffens and her hands come up to rest on my wrist but she doesn't push me away. She stares at the bunched cotton, dumbfounded and, for once, speechless. With swift precision, I tug her forward, bending my knees and throwing her over my shoulder.

The warmth of her skin against my hand and the brush of her hair on my arm as she thrashes around sends a surge of heat through me. Her fists hit my back, each thud only heightening my arousal. "Let me go, asshole."

Tightening my hold on her bare thighs, I can't help the sinful chuckle that falls from my lips. My strides are sure and even as I carry her back to our room.

Smoothing a hand up the back of her leg, I reply, "You're going to have to try harder than that, sweetheart."

"You're a thug and there isn't a reality in this universe where you willingly get a woman like me," she spits, her fists pummeling my back.

That's better. "And yet, here we are, in this universe with *my ring* on *your finger* as I carry *you* to *my bed.*"

If she thinks that she can spend a single night of our marriage in a bed other than mine, she's got another thing coming. I won't have my staff gossiping about the fact that my wife is sleeping as far from me as she can get.

"I won't ever let you lay a finger on me, you prick."

Her words send a flare of anger through my body, twisting with my arousal and urging me to show her who is in charge. "You seem to have forgotten who you're dealing with, *Mrs. Marino.*" I sneer.

Her body tenses, but she doesn't say another word.

When we reach our bedroom, I stalk into the space, throwing her down on the bed. She lands with a soft thud, my T-shirt riding up and giving me a glimpse of her black lacy underwear.

Margot sits up on her elbows but doesn't move to cover herself, and when I lift my eyes to hers, I see the challenge reflected in them.

A fire burns bright that tells me she's not done fighting.

Good.

Because neither am I.

Chapter 9

Margot

My eyes are wide, my chest rising and falling with every labored breath I pull in as I stare at Massimo towering over me. There's a charged energy crashing between us, and robbing any coherent thought from my mind. We're watching and waiting for the other to make a move and show their hand.

Massimo reaches for his belt buckle, his brown eyes stormy and unreadable as he uses one hand to undo it, the other fisted by his side. *Is he going to use that on me? A* thread of anticipation runs through me, robbing the air from my lungs. *Would I like it?*

I should tell him my secret.

The voice is quiet, barely audible over the rushing in my ears.

I should really tell him.

My lips part, my truth on the tip of my tongue

before I snap my mouth closed as Massimo says, "You're sorely mistaken if you think that we will be spending our marriage sleeping in separate rooms." He whips his belt through the loops of his trousers with such force that it cracks against the air before he drops it to the floor.

I'm transfixed, unable to rip my gaze away from his hands as they work on unzipping his pants and he closes the distance between us. "You are my *wife*." The way he says it, with such command, such possessiveness, it sends a thrill of need down my spine. "You will sleep in our bed. You will submit to *me*, Margot. Everything you do will be done to please *me* and you won't say a goddamn word about it."

I squeeze my legs together, anger, defiance, and arousal fighting for supremacy inside of me. "If you wanted that, you should have married someone—"

The air leaves me when Massimo wraps a hand around my ankle and drags me to the edge of the bed much like he did earlier. Except this time, with his pants undone and his intention clear, there's no denying what is going to happen.

He holds my legs to his chest and a sudden wave of nervousness washes over me. It ebbs when he smooths his warm hands over my thighs, the caress at odds with his words and brutal actions. Our eyes are still locked, his searching mine... for what, I don't know.

I should tell him.

Massimo fists my panties, snapping me out of whatever trance I was in. *What the hell does he think he's doing?* I grip his wrist in an effort to get him to release me.

"Get your hands off me," I spit, the anger in my heart colliding with the arousal fluttering in my stomach.

He smirks, his eyes darkening even as I dig my nails into his skin. With a practiced precision, he twists the material until it digs painfully into my flesh and snaps. I grimace, my eyes flooding with hot tears brought on by the pain. He doesn't bother to hide his arrogance; it's written in the smirk pulling at his full lips as he holds up the torn material, the fabric darkened from the dampness of my arousal.

Releasing him, I grip the sheets on either side of me and blow out a breath. I stare at the ceiling, refusing to look at him as unease rushes through me. Every instinct in me is screaming at me to push him away, to tell him no, but my body betrays me, falling limp and unmoving under his touch.

"Keep your eyes on me." His voice is a low and dangerous growl, but I don't comply.

I can't.

I can't show him my truth. If he see's how much I want him, he wins, and I'd rather die than face that truth. So I internalize it all, barely aware of Massimo's movements. I feel him shift my legs to hang over his forearms. I feel the pain shooting through my body as he lines up with my entrance and presses forward. I feel the way my body wants to welcome him inside.

My features pinch, and I turn my head to the side, a

tear falling from the corner of my eye and onto the sheet, the pain like nothing I've ever experienced before.

Massimo slams into me past the resistance of my virginity without hesitation. My back arches from the bed, my body tensing, and I cry out as all the air leaves my lungs at the unfamiliar intrusion. Under the veil of pain, nerve endings in my body I didn't know were there, spark to life. He holds still, the pads of his thumbs soothing the skin on my hips, but I don't seek him out. I'm not ready to let him take that final part of me. To see how he's so in control of my body that I crave his touch. *He can't have me.*

My chest rises and falls as I breathe around the burning sensation. It's like nothing I've ever felt before. Is he bigger than other guys? Would this have hurt as much if I'd lost my virginity to Ethan? My chest constricts at the reminder of him. It wouldn't have, because he'd have known what he was taking from me. *He'd have cherished it like a gift.*

"*Fuck me*, please tell me you weren't a virgin?" Massimo grits out.

Running a hand down my face, I wipe away the evidence of my pain. Schooling my features into a mask of indifference, as if I don't have my husband's cock—the only one I've ever experienced—buried inside of me, I finally look at him. "I think that's a pretty redundant question, given the fact that I am most definitely *not* anymore." Forcing my body to relax, I hold his stare and tilt my head as I ask, "Are you going to move or are we done?"

A muscle ticks in Massimo's jaw. He pulls back, and I brace myself, waiting for the pain to flare up. But what comes is nothing like the initial pain. There's a burn, but it's numbed by my arousal and a sense of loss as his cock leaves me. He drops my legs to the bed, stepping back with his clothes in disarray.

Of their own volition, my eyes dart down to Massimo's dick. It's hard and impossibly big with my blood covering it. The sight is something to behold. He lifts a hand, wrapping it around himself, and I watch, unable to tear my gaze away as he strokes himself from the base to the tip, using my blood and wetness as lubricant.

Sensing him watching me, I shift my focus to his face momentarily. His lips are slightly parted, and where I expect to see him mocking me, there's nothing but arousal swirling in his eyes. Still, heat fills my cheeks and I look away, staring at the moon sitting high in the sky beyond the window until his words draw my attention back to him.

"Did you see something you like?" he asks, lifting the hem of his top to reveal his defined abs.

I narrow my eyes and cross my arms over my chest. It's hard to come off as unfazed with my most intimate part on display for him. And yet, I don't want to give him any satisfaction in thinking that I want him. "Not really." I shrug. "Besides, I've seen better."

He cocks a brow, stepping closer to grip the front of

my T-shirt and force me up from the bed. "Yeah?" he snarls. "And who might that be? Because last time I checked, my cock is covered in your virgin blood."

There's a warning in his tone but apparently, I'm a fool and don't heed it. "Ethan, for one. And last time I checked, *dear husband*, just because I've not felt a cock in my pussy doesn't mean I haven't had one in my mouth or ass."

I haven't done the latter, but he doesn't need to know that.

I've tried things other than sex with Ethan, and I've had plenty of orgasms—mostly by my own hands.

A fire burns in his gaze, but I don't back down. *No.* I step into the flames, willing them to consume me. Massimo releases the cotton of my top, but I don't fall back, instead, I engage my core to stay upright.

We're inches apart as he lifts his hand and wraps it around my neck, applying a light pressure. He dips his head, his breath ghosting over my face as he pushes his forehead against mine. "Say it again, sweetheart."

Pressing forward until he must feel the pain that I do, I grit out, enunciating each word, "Ethan. For. One."

Massimo moves so quickly that I don't have time to think, let alone protest. He flips me over onto my stomach. The hand that was around my neck now pins me to the bed as he presses his lower body flush against mine, my ass exposed where my top has ridden up. The cotton of his trousers is smooth against my thighs but what draws my attention is the hot hardness of his still exposed cock that rests between my cheeks.

I don't know what he has planned and he doesn't give me any warning before his hand makes contact with my ass cheek. The sound echoes around the room colliding with my muffled cry. A sharp sting fills the flesh where he hit me but what surprises me is the rush of arousal that floods my core.

"Say. It. Again," Massimo growls.

I don't say a word, my shock rendering me speechless. *What is happening?* Out of the corner of my eye, I see Massimo draw his hand back. My body tenses, waiting for the contact but it doesn't come.

"That's what I thought," he snarls, dropping his hand.

Without another word, he lifts my hips, holding me steady as he pushes forward until he's filling me. My cries are muffled by the sheets beneath me. The pain is more bearable this time, dulled by an arousing ache as I stretch around him and my body accommodates his. I bite back the whimper of need that makes its way up my throat.

When he's fully seated inside of me, Massimo fists the material of my top again, pulling it back toward him and applying pressure to my neck with it. He shifts his hips back before driving forward, and a strangled moan slips free from my lips. It's half pleasure, half pain, my body pulsating around him, desperate for more.

"That will be the last time you speak his name in my house, Margot," Massimo spits, keeping his pace slow and deliberate as he fucks me.

My fingers grip the sheets, and I bite down on my bottom lip to keep from moaning and showing him how in control of my body he is.

Breathlessly, as if he's as close to the edge as I am, Massimo demands, "Understood?"

I don't respond, my thoughts unable to process anything but the feel of him and the energy racing through my body. *Why does it feel so good and yet wrong at the same time?* It shouldn't be him making me feel like this, it should be—

Massimo slaps my ass cheek as if he could sense where my thoughts had gone. "Never again, Margot," he grates through gritted teeth, as he picks up the pace and pounds into me with jerky movements.

Suddenly, he's gone and I'm left feeling empty. I fall forward as he releases his hold on me, my chest heaving as I suck in air.

He flips me onto my back and pulls me to the edge of the bed. With my legs once again over his forearms, he swipes his cock through my wet, aching pussy.

"You know how good this is, you can feel it. Hell, I felt it in the way your pussy spasmed around my cock when I slid inside you for the first time. If you want more, tell me you understand."

I bite down on my cheek, the pain a much needed distraction from the torture he's putting my body through. "No," I utter even as I writhe on the bed.

Massimo cocks a brow. "Then you leave me no choice," he drawls lazily, rubbing his thumb over my clit.

My back arches off the bed at the same time as my hips desperately buck, chasing a release. "No," I breathe, any conviction in my tone long gone.

"Your mouth is saying one thing but your body is saying something entirely different, Margot."

Aligning himself with my entrance, Massimo pushes forward in one smooth movement and my walls clench around him, pulling him in deeper. I can't contain the gasp of delight that rushes from my lips as he fills me. I wait for him to bring my body to nirvana, but he doesn't move.

"Massimo," I urge, the neediness foreign to my ears.

His fingers dig painfully into my thighs. "Tell. Me," he utters.

"I won't say his name." Desperation coats my words, and as soon as they are free from my lips, I regret them.

But that doesn't stop him. With my confirmation, he moves, sliding in and out of me with an exercised rhythm that stokes the embers inside of me. When he rubs his thumb over my clit, the flames are burning so hot that I'm certain he must feel my heat.

Before I know it, I'm arching my back and a wave of euphoria is crashing into me. Black dots appear on my vision, and I squeeze my eyes shut as my orgasm plows into me. My body convulses around Massimo, pulsating around his cock as I come undone.

I'm vaguely aware of him pulling out and spilling his cum onto my stomach. I feel him rubbing something through the mess, but I can't look. "'Til death do us part, Margot, and don't fucking forget it."

Reality crashes down on me and the truth of what just happened hits me. *I should never have allowed this.* The high of my orgasm vanishes, replaced by a crushing wave of guilt that makes my chest ache.

This wasn't just a mistake; it was a betrayal of everything I shared with Ethan.

Even though he has never made me feel the way Massimo just did.

It doesn't matter. Ethan has my heart, not Massimo. Ethan gave me my first orgasm and he was supposed to give me every one after.

Silently, I vow to myself that I won't let Massimo touch me again. I'll do everything in my power to keep him away. But even as my resolve sets in, there's a sliver of doubt coiling inside of me.

What if I'm not strong enough?

Chapter 10

Massimo

I mages of Margot beneath me as I fuck her flash through my mind like a cruel taunt, distracting me with every move. I've barely made it through my meetings today. She's occupied my mind, her scent still lingering on my skin, even after a shower. I've been in a constant state of arousal, my cock twitching, begging for more of her.

If I'd known how distracting she would be, I might've held back. But who am I kidding? The second her defiant eyes met mine, it was a done deal. *She's in my blood now.*

What I can't seem to wrap my head around is the fact that my spitfire of a wife was a fucking virgin. She's fucking addictive, and I barely know her.

There was never any question about us consummating our marriage, and I think after last night, she understands that ours will not be a sexless one.

"How does it feel?" Romeo asks, curiosity coating his

words and reminding me of where I am. He flew in two days ago with Aurora, his fiancée. As soon as we wrap up this meeting, he'll be joining her in New York City before they catch a flight back to Palermo.

I scrub a hand over my jaw as an image of Margot's bare ass bent over the bed with my cock covered in her juices resting between her cheeks flits through my mind.

A long exhale slips past my lips, and I move around my desk toward the drink trolley at the back of the room. It's only when I have my back to the others that I adjust myself. This can't go on. Being in a constant state of arousal while trying to talk business is only going to get me into trouble.

Clearing my throat, I focus my mind on the conversation and reply, "Being married? No different to the day before when I wasn't. My wife despises me, but she's not the first person to." Pouring out a glass of whiskey, I tip it back. It burns as it travels through my body before settling like a comforting warmth in the pit of my stomach.

Refilling the glass, I drop back onto the couch beside the trolley and cross my ankle over my knee. Staring at the four imposing men around me, I continue, "I'm sure you want to get back to Aurora, Rome. Let's get down to business. Daniele, what do you have for us?"

Daniele shrugs, cracking his neck. "We're no closer to finding Anastasia. Our contacts are either unwilling to talk or unable to talk. I hate to say it, but I think they might be more afraid of her than they are of us."

"So we're nowhere?" Romeo grinds out.

Daniele opens the manila folder and spreads out the grainy images across the table. "We got these from a building near the raid site." He points to a blonde woman in a baseball cap. "Aurora's description matches. It's her."

"Is there any more footage from the surrounding area?"

"Yes, but then it's like she disappears into thin air. Our contacts in the police department are keeping us updated on their side of things, but unless we can get more eyes on this, she could avoid us for months."

I dart a look at Leonardo. I can't force him to return home. He needs to find Haven; it's imperative that we bring her back, if not for her own sake, then for Maria, my head housekeeper and also her mother. "Bring Aldo into the fold. We need to find her, if only to close this down."

"You think you can trust him?" Romeo asks.

I consider his question. Trust is a fragile currency in our world and not something that should be taken for granted. Especially where one wrong move could be the end of us. But it's been weeks since the last attack, and right now, it feels like we need to throw caution to the wind before we run out of time.

I take a sip of my drink, leaning back into the cushions and leveling Romeo with my stare. "It's not without risks, but he's worked for our family for longer than either of us has been alive. Hell, he has more connections than all of us put together and we should have brought him in from day one. Besides, I'm sure Daniele is eager to get home."

Romeo stares at me before nodding and replying, "If you think that's for the best, then brief him and bring him into the fold."

I don't need his approval—he knows that—but given what happened to Aurora and the fact that somebody in *my house* is either behind it or helped with it, well, this is the least I can do.

Leaning forward, I rest my elbows on my knees and turn my attention to Leonardo. "How's the search for Haven coming?"

His tired eyes hold mine for a beat before he looks down, shaking his head. "Pretty much the same as Daniele's for Anastasia," Leonardo explains, his voice thick with exhaustion. "She's better at hiding than I gave her credit for, but with an unborn baby to protect..." He trails off, dragging his hand down his face. "Christ, I don't blame her for running."

His words linger in the air, drowning us in regret as guilt settles like a stone in the pit of my stomach. For the first time in all the time I've known him, I see the cracks in Leonardo's armor.

We fucked up.

I fucked up.

I'll be the first to admit that, but I gave the order based on the evidence we had. Everything pointed toward Haven, but now we know that was because of the rat. CCTV showed Haven answering a call that appeared to come from the Russians.

It wasn't until Aurora returned and confirmed what Haven had said that I realized my mistake. By then, it was too late. Now, she's pregnant, on the run and no doubt afraid, but wallowing in our regret won't solve our problems, and right now, we need to focus on surviving rather than redemption.

We can beg for forgiveness once we make it out of this mess alive.

Restlessness claws at me, fighting to find its way out. It's been there ever since Massimo dragged me back to his room last night and took what wasn't his to take. He showed me a glimpse of what he's capable of; of the monster who will take whatever he wants without asking or thinking twice about it.

And the worst part? I've spent all the time since it happened replaying every second. Reliving the way he played my body like an instrument and it betrayed me in the most heinous way. *I hate how much I enjoyed it.*

Heat coils under my skin; hot and commanding. Marching across the room, I storm into the corridor, my chest heaving with the restless urgency that races through me. *I need to get out of this room.*

Crossing the threshold, I come to a stop in the corridor, listening to the sounds of the house. I catch my reflection in the window, studying how my shoulders are tense and my eyes wide and unblinking. *I feel wild.*

In the distance, I see the trees lining the driveway, their leaves a vibrant green from the rain earlier in the morning. I blow out a breath, forcing my body to relax but no sooner has some of the tension ebbed away, it returns with full force.

I shake out my body before closing my eyes and inhaling a lungful of air. My nostrils are assaulted by a chemically lemon scent left behind by whatever cleaning products have been used.

This time, when I blow out my breath, it's like a calm has washed over me, at least on the surface. Underneath though, there's still a current running through me. It matches the energy of the house, humming with dark secrets I have no right or desire to uncover; it makes me feel *alive.*

My bare feet are silent as I pad down the hallway, determined to explore my new home. The polished floors are cool against the soles of my feet and the dim lighting only emphasizes the coldness.

Will this place ever really be a home?

I don't think so. For as long as I'm forced to live here, married to a man who thinks he can have his own way with every aspect of my life, this place will be my prison.

Massimo's house is as imposing as the man himself. Despite the paintings adorning them, the stark white walls feel clinical. Endless hallways wind to places I'm yet to explore, but what gets me the most is how the house breathes. Like it knows I'm here under protest and thrives on it.

When I reach the end of the corridor, I hesitate, listening for any sign of movement. Somewhere in the distance, I hear voices, but I can't tell where they're coming from. Every sound seems to bounce off the walls and reverberate around me.

I stand tall, lifting my chin before I force myself to continue moving. I need to know this house as well as my enemy does, especially if I want to hold on to any hope of surviving my time here.

———

I've been wandering the halls for thirty minutes when I eventually stumble upon the library. My sigh of contentment is palpable as I walk into the room. After a dozen locked doors and nearly as many empty spaces, it's refreshing to see a room actually have a purpose.

The library is a world away from the rest of the house; it's almost sacred in its comfort. For a moment, I imagine what it would be like to curl up with a book and get lost in a world of fantasy, one that doesn't have the threat of danger looming around every corner.

Books line two of the four walls with an empty desk in front of one at the back. Two oversized leather armchairs and a matching couch surround an open fireplace, and although the room has *things* in it, it doesn't look like it's utilized. The thought has an ache settling in my chest, heavy and suffocating. *It feels like such a waste.*

Pressing a hand over my heart, I move around the room wishing away the feeling. It has no place in my emotions, not now anyway.

"Curiosity will get you killed. Did nobody ever tell you that it's a very dangerous habit to have?" The voice cuts through the quiet, slightly accented, smooth and low.

I whirl around, my eyes wide and my heart pounding in my chest. A man stands in the doorway, blocking the only exit. His tall frame is silhouetted by the corridor's lighting, giving him an almost sinister backdrop.

For the first time since I was forced to come here, I feel a thread of terror weave its way down my spine. Considering who I have just married, the realization clogs the air in my lungs, making it hard to breathe.

His hair is dark but streaked with gray and the smile doesn't quite reach his eyes. My brows tug together. Whoever he is, he carries himself with an air of importance. It's obvious in his imposing frame as he leans against the doorjamb with one hand in his pocket. Where Massimo is fire, this man is ice. I'm just not sure which might be worse.

He must be an important figure in Massimo's operation. *If he's that important, why didn't I see him at the wedding?*

The thought is nearly laughable. There were over two hundred people at our wedding and I knew ten of them. *No.* This guy is *somebody*, that much I know.

His cold gaze lingers a fraction too long, as though he's cataloging any weakness I dare to show and filing it away to use against me at a later date. I resist the urge to step back and put some distance between us. "I'm sorry, is this your room?" My voice comes out sharper than I intend, tarnished with a hint of accusation.

"Not at all," he says, pushing away from the frame and stepping further into the room. "Every room in this house is yours now, is it not? At least that's what they'll tell you." He prowls toward me, his words laced with amusement.

My curiosity is piqued, but I keep my expression neutral. Something tells me that even if I voiced the question on the tip of my tongue, he wouldn't give me an answer. This guy keeps his cards close to his chest, I can tell that much about him, even if everything else is unreadable.

"Aldo." He comes to a stop in front of me, holding out his hand. Without missing a beat—because I'll be damned if I show any weakness—I slip my hand into his. His grip is firm, but it's the way his eyes study me, like I'm a specimen under a microscope. It sets me on edge even more than I already am. "Massimo's *consigliere*. His right-hand man."

"Margot," I reply, pulling my hand back and walking around the desk toward the armchairs to put some space between us.

"I know. The *new* Mrs. Marino. Your marriage to Massimo has caused quite a stir." He circles the desk following the path I just took. His movements are slow and deliberate, like a hunter trailing his prey. Fear skates down my spine, lifting the hairs on the back of my neck. "Let me give you some friendly advice, Margot." I grit my teeth at the underlying threat in his tone, tilting my head as I feign nonchalance and wait for him to continue. "If you are going to survive as Massimo's wife, there are certain rules you should abide by and certain places you should stay out of."

I hold his gaze, refusing to cower, like I'm certain he either wants or expects me to. My heart races in the confines of my chest. "Thanks for the advice, but I think I'll be okay." The corner of my mouth lifts, and I wait for him to make his next move.

His jaw works as he levels me with a stare, something I can't quite identify swimming in the depths of his almost black eyes. "Don't say I didn't warn you, Margot." There's a detached coldness to his tone that speaks volumes of his nature.

I straighten my spine and watch him as he leaves the room. It's only when I'm certain that he's gone that I relax and drop into the armchair behind me.

Staring out of the window, I watch a murder of crows swoop through the sky before they take shelter from the light rain in a nearby tree. I never thought I'd look forward to Massimo coming home, but something about that interaction with Aldo has left me feeling unsettled.

As much as I hate to admit it, the house feels a little less dangerous with Massimo in it.

Chapter 12

Margot

I'm in the kitchen when I feel his presence. Every muscle in my body tenses in anticipation before I've even laid eyes on Massimo. It's been a week since we became intimately tied to each other, but he hasn't touched me since. I'm grateful for that, but every day that passes only makes the tension gnawing in my gut coil tighter.

I keep my eyes fixed on the dish in front of me, my appetite long gone. His energy is undeniable, feeding into me and making my heart race. And yet, he moves around the kitchen with ease, unknowing of the reaction he's caused in me as he chats with Alma, his chef, in hushed tones before heading in my direction.

Carefully and with a false calmness, I place my napkin on the table and stand, pushing my chair back. When he takes a seat at the head of the table, I fight to control my reaction to his proximity, keeping it locked up inside and refusing to show my turmoil at wanting to beg him to touch me or scream at him for doing what he's doing to me.

"Sit." It's a command that has my body obediently dropping back into my chair.

What is wrong with me? The embers of a fire inside of me spark to life. I will not obey him. He is not my master and I am not his puppet. Standing again, I push my chair back, the legs scraping across the tiled floor, loud and brash in the otherwise quiet room. Massimo glances at me, one brow raised. His cold, hard stare holds a challenge, waiting for me to push back so he can... *punish me?* I won't give him the satisfaction.

My eyes bounce around his face searching for a sign that he's going to tell me this whole thing—our marriage, the way he took my virginity, the control he has over me—was all a dream. Better yet, that it was all a sick prank and I can go back to my *normal* life. But I see nothing. No hint at what game he's playing or how long he expects us to do... *this.* Defeated, I slump back into my seat, and stare at the ceiling.

"You know, this would go a lot smoother if you didn't act like such a child, Margot." He takes a sip of his espresso, his eyes boring into me over the edge of the cup.

Rolling my head on the back of my chair, I regard him and the finger that is bare of his wedding band before I drawl, "Here's an idea. Find a different wife? Unless taking women who can't stand you and don't want you is what turns you on?"

The wolfish smirk that transforms his face as his mouth lifts up on one side has my pulse racing with desire, and yet my head is screaming at me to run. To put distance between us. Instead, I stay put, refusing to show him any weakness, because that's what my attraction to him is.

"Why would I want anyone else when I have *you*?" He pauses, waiting for me to answer, but when I refuse to speak, he continues, "The way I see it, Margot, you have two choices."

I scoff, blown away at the fact that he thinks I have *choices*. Sitting up straighter, I tilt my head and lean into him. "Do you really believe that I have a choice in this situation? Are you that delusional?"

He moves so quickly that I don't have time to react. His hand is warm, firm, and commanding as he wraps it around the nape of my neck. My pulse thuds against his fingers, the buds of my nipples pebbling in the cups of my bra and betraying the anger I've been trying so hard to hold on to. I lift my head, meeting his eyes with a glare that I pray masks the war of frustration and need waging inside of me.

Massimo presses his forehead against mine. "Watch how you speak to me, Margot. There's a thin between you living a comfortable life here and ending up buried in the ground."

Heat prickles my skin and my heart hammers against my rib cage as unease washes through me at his statement. And yet, an undercurrent of excitement pulses through me at the thought of him touching me again, at the danger he clearly exudes. Pulling back as much as he will allow me, I inject boredom into my tone when I reply, "So my choices are to either be married to you or be killed?"

Releasing me, Massimo leans back in his chair, picking up his espresso and finishing it before he provides me with an answer. I track his movements, shifting in my seat as I stare at his large hands, the veins flexing and rippling as he moves. "No. Your choices are to make the best out of this situation or carry on as you are. If you choose the latter, it's only *you* that will suffer."

Blinking, I force my eyes to meet his. I cross my arms over my chest, biting the inside of my mouth when his eyes flit to my cleavage. "And how do you propose I make the best out of this *terrible* situation?" I huff.

Massimo lifts a shoulder before dropping it. "We can start with getting to know each other."

An incredulous giggle slips from my mouth before I clamp it shut. I stare at him with wide eyes. "Sorry, but that's what you're supposed to do *before* you get married."

Massimo sighs, running his tongue over his teeth as an idea forms in my mind, sending a rush of excitement through me.

"Okay, I'll try it your way." I rest my elbows on the oak table, tucking my hands under my chin as I inject as much sweetness into my tone as I can muster. "Dearest husband."

Massimo's eyes drop to my mouth, something sinful

swirling in their depths. I wait for his gaze to return to mine.

Tilting my head to the side, I stare into his almost black eyes and ask, "How many men have you killed?"

His eyes hold mine, searching for something that he doesn't find. "I have no issue telling you that number, Margot, but when I do, you can't take that knowledge back."

Blinking, I let out a slow breath. I don't really want to know. It's not going to change anything and get me out of this marriage. If anything, it's going to cement my connection to him and that's the last thing I want. "Fine, don't tell me. What do you want to know about me?"

"I'll start with an easy one. What did you do for work before?" He moves his finger back and forth between us. *Before I was forced into our marriage.*

I settle back into my chair, folding my arms over my chest. "That's what you want to talk about? Okay." Inhaling, I sigh, "I didn't have a job."

His brows pull together, and for the first time since we met, I think I see something akin to disappointment flare in his gaze. "You're twenty-two. What happened with your last job?"

Heat blooms in my chest, traveling up my neck and flaming my face. "I've never had a job. I was in education, and when that finished, I was trying to figure out what I wanted to do."

"What were you studying?"

I release a chuckle, looking around the room. "It

doesn't matter now. It's not like I'll have the opportunity to do anything with it."

Massimo stares at me, the weight of his focus almost unbearable. "I don't plan on keeping you locked up like a prisoner, Margot. If there is something you want to do and it doesn't conflict with what we do here, then you are free to pursue it."

A hush falls over the kitchen, the only sounds coming from somewhere else in the house. It's only now that I realize we're alone. I was so ensnared by him that I didn't even notice Alma had left the room.

Needing something else to focus on besides the fact that there is nothing stopping Massimo from doing what he wants to me on this table, I say, "How long have you been..." My question trails off, unsure of whether or not I can acknowledge what he does.

He fills in my blanks. "I've been the head of this family—at least the American side of things—for the last ten years. I worked with my father for a while before he got sick and then I took over with him on the sidelines, providing me with guidance until he passed."

There's something about knowing Massimo had family that makes him seem almost human. *Almost.* I'd be a fool to forget the monster beneath the polished surface. My voice is flat and devoid of any emotion, just as intended, when I reply, "I'm sorry for your loss."

He shrugs, like losing a parent is no big deal. "It was a long time ago." We fall quiet for a moment before he asks, "Tell me, why don't you get on with your mother?"

I scoff, narrowing my eyes. "What makes you think that I don't?"

Leaning back in his chair, he rests an arm on the table, drawing my attention to the corded muscles. "It doesn't take a genius to put two and two together. Even with our limited interactions before we got married, I could feel the bubble of tension between you." He falls quiet for a moment, but when I don't speak, he continues, "So, why do you not get along with your mother?"

I tear my gaze away, staring at the swirling pattern in the table top before I reply, "That's the understatement of the century. Josephine is..." I pause, unsure if I should be so vocal with a man like Massimo about her. He stares at me, no judgment in his gaze, just waiting for me to continue. "Josephine is a unique person, but growing up with her as my sole parent was hard. She can give you whiplash. One minute she's a doting mother and I'm her 'baby girl' and the next, when a man comes along, I'm forgotten about, left to fend for myself. It was easier to detach my emotions when it comes to her than to keep on the ride."

Something flits through Massimo's gaze, but it's gone so quickly that I can't name it. I tear my eyes away from him, wondering if I've shared too much.

Staring at my hands, I prepare to stand when he speaks again. "What do you do for fun?"

I huff out a laugh at his change in subject, relief flooding me. Lifting my gaze to him, I reply, "I like to read and I go out with my friends, usually shopping or to a club."

"What do you read?" Genuine curiosity floods his expression.

"Anything. If it interests me, I'll read non-fiction but my favorites are the classics, like Emily Bronte, Harper Lee, and Charles Dickens." I shrug, his unfiltered intrigue in me stirring something in my gut.

Massimo opens his mouth to speak but closes it again when his phone vibrates on the table. Picking it up, he checks the screen before swiping to unlock it. "I have to go. I'll be in my office if you need anything."

And just like that, he's gone, leaving behind the faint scent of his cologne and my body tingling with a neediness I have no hope of satiating.

I'd do well to remember that this isn't a traditional marriage; this is a minefield. It's a landscape where I'll be forever trying to dodge the attraction I feel for my husband as we each fight our battles to win the war. And I'm sure that right now, Massimo thinks I'll surrender if he just gets me to open up, but he's mistaken.

I'm just getting started.

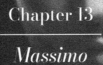

Chapter 13

Massimo

It's one in the morning by the time I head for bed, the quiet of the house making my thoughts louder than ever. We've had to change around our operations since the attacks and inevitably this has led to more work. It doesn't help that I have the heads of the other four families in the tri-state area up my ass about debuting my fucking wife. I plan on putting that off as long as possible and at least until Margot is less...*hostile.*

I cross the threshold into the pitch-black bedroom, leaving the door slightly ajar to guide me as I move through the space. There's no denying that she's in here this time, even though I can barely make out her sleeping form. Her sweet fragrance fills the air, reminding me of our wedding night.

Scrubbing a hand over my face, I smother my yawn before quietly undressing. Exhaustion has become a constant in my life these past few weeks, but it doesn't mean it gets any easier.

Folding my clothes, I leave them on the chair in the corner, my aching body begging me to fall into the comfort of my bed. I know as soon as my head hits the pillow, I'll be asleep.

Pulling back the covers, I go to climb in, my knee resting on the mattress when Margot's phone vibrates across her nightstand. I freeze as the screen lights up, illuminating the room and her sleeping features.

My eyes remain locked on the device long after the screen has gone black and it's only when it lights up again that I move around to her side. She's my wife now. My responsibility. If someone is texting her at one in the morning, I need to know what it's about. My eyes dart to Margot before I pick up her phone and wake up the screen.

ETHAN

New Message

Every muscle in my body tenses, my jaw grinding as I think over my next move. I consider dragging her to the basement and making good on the threats I've given. She should have heeded my warnings because now she'll only have herself to blame for the consequences of her actions.

And she will pay for this betrayal.

I don't need to see what he has said to know that. The simple fact that he's still communicating with her is enough. Still, I tap on the message and when the screen requests the passcode, I enter it. Any ounce of guilt I carried at having Callum get it for me is washed away.

With the message thread filling the screen, I scroll up to the messages they've exchanged since she broke it off with him, the date engrained in my memory.

ETHAN

I don't understand what's happening, Margot. Are you in danger? Is that why you did what you did? I thought you loved me.

MARGOT

I'm so sorry, Ethan. I wish I could tell you more.

ETHAN

Talk to me. We can figure this out. Whatever is happening, I'll help fix it if it means we can be together.

MARGOT

That's not possible. Please, don't make this any harder than it has to be, Ethan. You'll find someone else and forget about me.

ETHAN

I never thought, when you made me promise to remember how much I loved you, that you'd rip my heart out seconds later, M.

It's been less than twenty-four hours since you did and I miss you like crazy. There isn't a universe in which we both exist that I could ever forget about you.

Before reading on, I glance at Margot, her features

softened by sleep and her lips parted as she draws in quiet breaths. She looks untouched by the chaos she's caused, her betrayal lying still beneath the surface like a dormant volcano.

Does she know I'm standing here, fighting the urge to wake her and demand answers? Is she dreaming of him and the life she could have had? I grind my teeth together at the thought, a hot burning sensation burning through my chest as I try to contain my anger.

Redirecting my focus to the phone in my hand, I tighten my grip and read on.

MARGOT

I wish I could tell you what was happening. I wish I didn't miss you as much as I do. I wish we'd run away.

His response is almost instantaneous, like he's still holding on to some form of hope that he can say the right thing and get her back.

ETHAN

We can. Wherever you want to go, we'll go. Just tell me when and where to meet you and I'll be there.

I love you, Margot. If you're in danger, I'll do everything I can to protect you.

MARGOT

I wish it was that simple, but there isn't anything you can do.

I scroll through more messages, each one only fanning the flames of my fury. The beast inside of me, the one that I only unleash on my worst enemies, fights to be released. I reach the end of the chain, reading over her last message.

MARGOT

> I don't deserve your forgiveness or your support, but you're the only one who really knows me. My wedding is on Saturday, at St. Bart's on Park Avenue. The ceremony starts at 12 noon. I really would like you to come.

I sigh heavily, continuing to scroll until I reach the bottom of the thread, ignoring the messages that he's sent to her without a response. Her only saving grace right now is that it at least *looks* like she's not been speaking to him since the wedding, but I'd be a fool to not have Callum pull her phone data. I won't put it past her to be deleting messages.

ETHAN

> Please call me, I need to know that you're okay. That he hasn't done something to you. I love you.

> I just need the address and I'm there.

Deleting the last two messages, I lock her phone and slide it back onto the nightstand. I stare down at her sleeping form, barely illuminated by the light spilling into the room from the doorway.

The anger simmering in my chest doesn't dissipate, it only heightens as the seconds tick by. Tomorrow, Ethan will learn what happens when you try to take something that belongs to me.

And Margot? She'll understand that there's no escaping this.

No escaping *me*.

Chapter 14

Massimo

With every step I take along the dingy corridor of Ethan's apartment building, the messages he exchanged with *my wife* flash through my mind, taunting me and fueling my wrath. The overhead lights in the hallway flicker, like they know what's coming and are trying to send a signal. But in truth, *I can't be stopped.*

My fury has been simmering beneath the surface all night and now that I'm here, it's ready to erupt. I use my thumb to twist my wedding band round on my finger. The metal feels foreign but is a heavy reminder of the commitment Margot has betrayed. I will ensure that Ethan has no doubts about who Margot belongs to before I leave.

The power of my anger surges through my fist as I pound on the wood of Ethan's apartment door. It vibrates the walls, and on the other side, I hear his urgency as he rushes to see who it is.

Covering the peephole, I wait for him to answer, smirking when he inevitably opens the door a crack, leaving the chain connected to the frame.

Wide, dull brown eyes peer through the gap. *Ethan Watkins.* The fear branded into his expression is a sight I thrive on. It collides with the excitement thrumming through my veins.

He gasps before trying to shut me out, but he's too slow. I wedge my foot in the gap, and when his lips part in surprise, I take his momentary distraction to slam my body against the door. The chain breaks, wood splintering and flying through the air. It follows Ethan as he stumbles backward, landing with a thump on the scuffed laminate flooring.

Crossing the threshold, I kick what's left of the door closed behind me, pulling out a pair of black gloves from my pocket. As I slide them on, I look around his apartment, my lip curling, not bothering to hide my disgust. I can see everything, the half-wall separating the kitchen from the rest of the apartment essentially useless.

The fact that he thought a beauty as *magnificent* as Margot's would belong in a shithole like this only infuriates me further. I growl, baring my teeth, unable to contain my emotions any longer. When I take a step toward him, he shuffles back, not having the wits about him to stand and face me like a man. I don't know what Margot saw in him. *He's weak and pathetic.*

"W-w-whatever you want, I'll do it," Ethan stutters, confirming my thoughts.

Each step I take is measured and exudes an air of calm. It's in direct contrast to the disorder beneath the surface, but he'll see that soon enough if he doesn't tell me what I want to hear. Running my tongue over my teeth, I stare down at him, my arrogance stifling. "If that were the case, I wouldn't be here."

He comes to a stop against the half-wall and I crouch down so that we're somewhat eye to eye. I let my expectation for an answer to my unvoiced question hang between us until he splutters, "I don't know what I was thinking. I'm sorry. I won't talk to her anymore, I promise."

Standing, I shrug out of my jacket and throw it over the couch before removing my knife from the inside pocket. I stride toward the table and chairs neatly tucked away under the window. I lift one of them, setting it down in the middle of the cramped room.

"Sit," I command, pointing to the couch with my knife, my tone brokering no argument.

The familiar scent of fear fills the air. Ethan scrambles from the floor, his eyes darting to the door for a moment before he reconsiders whatever foolish idea floated through his mind. He lowers himself onto the cushions, a slight tremor wracking his body.

Taking a seat in front of him, I roll up the sleeves of my black button-down shirt and force my body to relax. "What do you know about me?"

He swallows, his Adam's apple bobbing with the action as he works to hide the flare of surprise in his gaze. "Not much."

I press my lips together, irritation adding an edge to my tone. "Humor me. What do you know?"

With his eyes on a point over my shoulder, he exhales and says, "I know you own a club and your family is... allegedly involved in the mafia."

I lean forward, running the knife over his knee before pressing the point into the flesh of his thigh. With the barrier of his clothes and the light but firm pressure I'm applying, it won't do much damage. *Unless I want it to.* His body goes rigid.

"So you know enough. What I don't understand is why you're still in contact with her. Knowing who I am—because, let's be honest, there's no '*allegedly*' about it— why have you not left her alone?"

He lifts his chin, a determination shining in his gaze as if the idea of her gives him strength. "She—"

I apply more pressure to the knife, his flesh giving way under the force. Blood seeps into the fabric of his jeans and his words turn into a hissed breath. He flinches from the pain and liquid pools in his eyes before he sniffs and sets his jaw.

"When you give me your answer, remember who I am, and who *she* is to *me—my wife*. Not who she *was* to you." My voice is deceptively soft, but the threat is clear.

Ethan nods, a muscle in his jaw working. "I don't know why," he rasps.

Clicking my tongue, I lean back, removing the knife from his flesh. "That's disappointing. I'm sure you do know why, but I guess when faced with the reality of your circumstances, you're choosing to be a coward." Standing, I stare down at him, tilting my head before I continue, "I thought my wife would have better taste than that."

I see the fight return to him, but he bites his tongue, choosing to live over fighting me. Sliding the knife into my pants pocket, I demand, "Where's your phone?"

Ethan drops his chin to his chest, mumbling, "On the nightstand."

It takes me seconds to cross the space and grab it up. I return to him, grabbing a fistful of his hair and forcing his head back. I hold the phone up, waiting for the telltale click to confirm it's unlocked using facial recognition before pushing his head back. Bringing up the text chain with Margot, I type out a message.

> ETHAN
>
> Don't contact me again. You're married and made a commitment to your husband. You should be honoring it, not messaging a man you can no longer have.

I press send, block Margot's number, and delete her contact information. It does little to ease my frustration. Throwing his phone onto the couch beside him, I wait for Ethan to meet my gaze before delivering my final message. "You got lucky this time, but if you try to contact Margot again, I'll be back and your family will be sent pieces of you in the mail. Got it?"

He swallows thickly, nodding. "Yes, sir."

Without looking back, I march from his apartment, the energy I came with barely satiated. Ethan may have learned his lesson, at least for now, but there's still Margot to deal with. She needs a reminder of the vows she swore to me, and tonight, I'll remind her of the meaning of the word loyalty.

Chapter 15

Margot

Unblinking, I stare at the ceiling, my temples damp from the tears I couldn't hold back when I first read Ethan's message. His words were like a stab to the heart and severed any hope of me ever earning his forgiveness.

I guess he couldn't keep that promise, after all.

A sob lodges itself in my throat, choking me as tears stream down into my hairline. *This can't be real.* A heaviness settles into the pit of my stomach and nausea washes through me.

I close my eyes, biting down on my bottom lip to keep quiet. Hours have passed and I haven't been able to move, paralyzed by my grief. The loss of him feels both gut-wrenching and numbing at the same time and yet I *knew* this would happen. That eventually I would lose him. *I just didn't think it would be this soon.*

Sitting up, I rest against the headboard and bring my

knees to my chest. With my cheek resting on them, I stare out of the window, watching as the breeze ruffles the leaves and a lone bird sweeps through the darkened sky. I haven't been able to bring myself to respond to him yet. *What would I even say?*

A knock at the door cuts through the silence but I don't move. *I can't.* At my lack of answering, the door opens, the china rattling on a tray an indication of who it is.

"Margot," Maria, Massimo's head housekeeper, calls tentatively. When I don't move or respond, she continues, "Alma said you hadn't been down for breakfast. We thought it might be a good idea to bring you something to eat."

She places the tray on the nightstand, before smoothing her hand over my head. I close my eyes to ease the stinging sensation brought on by her tenderness. Josephine would never have shown such a maternal gesture. Hell, it's because of her—and Alvin—that I'm in this situation.

"Please eat something. Alma and I will be downstairs if you need us." She hesitates for a moment, as if she knows her next words will be ones I won't care for. "Massimo called to say he won't be back for dinner."

Good.

I have no doubt that my husband is behind Ethan's message in some way or another. Whether that is because he invaded my privacy and went through my phone or because his reputation precedes him, it doesn't matter. I have no desire to see him or breathe the same air as him.

When Maria leaves, I unfurl myself and shuffle further under the covers. Inhaling sharply, I unlock my phone and type out a short and to the point message.

MARGOT

Did he get to you?

God, I sound paranoid. Deleting the text, I try again.

MARGOT

What's happened?

I press send, biting the skin on the side of my thumb as I wait for it to deliver. Nerves flutter in my stomach like a kaleidoscope of butterflies. It feels like an eternity before a red X appears next to the message with two little words, *not delivered*, tipping my world on its axis. *Has he blocked me?*

There isn't a world in this universe where *my* Ethan would block me. This is all on Massimo. It has to be. He made his threats and I was foolish enough to think he wouldn't find out that we were still communicating. But if I'm the reason that something has happened to Ethan, I don't know how I'll ever live with myself.

Fuck Massimo.

Fuck him and Alvin for dragging me into this mess.

Throwing the covers off, I march into the bathroom and switch on the shower. If Massimo thinks he has

control over me, maybe it's about time that I showed him
how little control he actually has.

As I wait for the water to get hot, I bring up the group
chat with my best friends, Reagan and Cece. We've
known each other since we were in diapers. They're my
ride or die.

MARGOT

I need to get drunk. Are you in?

Putting my phone on the sink unit, I undress,
throwing my pajamas into the laundry basket. Even if
Reagan and Cece aren't up for getting drunk, I'm still
going out. Besides, who knows what Massimo is up to.
For all I know, he could be out there screwing another
woman. He said our marriage wouldn't be a sexless one
and yet he hasn't touched me in a week, and I'm not
naive enough to think that he isn't beyond getting his
needs satisfied elsewhere.

I shower quickly, wrapping a towel around my body
and checking my phone to see if I've had a response
when I step out of the cubicle. A smile pulls at the corner
of my mouth when I read through their messages.

REAGAN

You don't need to ask me twice.

CECE

Bitch, you ghosted us, so drinks are
on you!

REAGAN

I don't think she had a choice in that...

CECE

She's still paying.

REAGAN

Duh! It's the least she can do.

Are you reading this, Margs? You
owe us.

You would have thought I'd ghosted them for years and that they weren't in my bridal party a week ago.

MARGOT

I've kinda had other things to deal
with...

REAGAN

We forgive you but you need to fill us in
tonight. Preferably before we get sloppy
drunk!

CECE

Pick you up at eight. We'll grab a hotel
in the city for tonight but be ready to go
straight to the club.

P.S. We missed you.

Returning to the bedroom, I throw my phone onto the bed before flopping down onto it. I have five hours until we leave, which is plenty of time to eat and get ready. I might be angry at Massimo but I'm not going to punish myself with the hangover of hell tomorrow because I didn't want to eat his food.

———

It turns out, five hours was not a lot of time. I'm late and still have to get to the end of the driveway to meet the girls. Not forgetting the fact that I have to sneak out of this place because I'm fairly certain that Massimo would have wanted to send someone to babysit me and I don't need that ruining my night.

Creeping down the hallway, I flinch with every creak of the floorboards under my feet. For all I know, someone could be watching my every move on hidden cameras, but I will not be stopped. The house is quiet but somehow it feels too loud and every shadow has the potential to expose me.

I reach the top of the staircase and with my hand on the banister for support, I navigate the steps in my six-inch sparkly silver stilettos. It doesn't help that I started drinking double rum and cokes as I was getting ready. Here's hoping Massimo doesn't mind that I stole it from the bar in the lounge, but I figured a little Dutch courage would help with the whole 'breaking out of a mafia mansion' thing, but it's probably just going to hinder me. Especially as with every step I take closer to the front door, it seeps further into my blood.

When I reach the bottom step, I blow out a relieved breath before straightening the twin slits of my flowing black skirt and making sure nothing else is on show in the revealing dress.

I've had to forgo underwear for fashion tonight, but I feel sexy and like I might just cause a riot, so it's worth it. The daring cutouts, high slits on the front and back, and the plunging halter neckline leave little to the imagination. I'm sure it will piss Massimo off and that makes goosebumps of anticipation form on the exposed skin at my waist.

"Going somewhere?" Daniele asks, his voice low and calm, slicing through the quiet.

I whip around, my heart pounding as I watch him emerge from the shadows, an apple in his hand and a smirk on his face.

Damn it.

"You scared me." My brain works a mile a minute to formulate a plan, but I give up, instead blurting out, "I'm going out. Don't wait up."

He cocks a brow, biting into his apple and slowly chewing on it. "Yeah?" he asks around a mouthful of fruit.

"Yes." I widen my eyes, before tossing my perfectly curled hair over my shoulder, and marching across the entryway toward the front door. Maybe if I give off an air of self-importance, he won't question my plans. At least that's what I tell myself.

"I take it Massimo knows you're going? And he's arranged security for you?"

I freeze mid-stride, my body tensing before I exhale. Pulling open the door, I call over my shoulder, "Of course."

Liar.

"One last question, before you leave." *It feels like a trap.* Keeping my back to him, I ignore the pounding of my pulse in my ears and wait. "Where are you going? And who has he sent with you?"

Okay. *This is easy.* Turning, I fix a serene smile on my lips and say, "That's two questions." I throw him a wink, my hand ready to open the closed door and be on my way. "I'm going to Aces." *The lies are really flowing freely tonight.* I know that Massimo owns Aces and I really hope that Daniele will let me leave without any more questions because I have no intention of stepping foot in his club.

He studies me down his nose, his eyes narrowed and assessing. The weight of his stare is heavy and makes me feel uncomfortable.

When he doesn't speak, I take a step, opening the door. "Okay." I drag out the word. "Well, this has been fun."

As I go to leave, Daniele moves, and on the periphery of my vision, I see his hand grab the edge of the door and pull it back. I stumble back, moving with the door where I hold the handle, my reflexes too slow to react and release it. The sound of my hand slapping against the wood to keep myself upright echoes around the entry-way. I hiss through clenched teeth at the pain that travels the length of my arm.

Unfazed, Daniele cups my elbow, waiting for me to straighten before he releases me and holds the door open wider. Waving his hand in front of himself, he says, "After you."

Panic flares in my chest, blowing my eyes wide and I

rasp, "Where are we going?" My mind races to figure out a plan to get away from him.

Daniele looks at me expectantly, before sighing heavily and replying, "To Aces. I have a meeting with Massimo. Your friends." He looks in the direction of the main gate. "Have been told to meet you there."

I exhale, relief seeping into my bones. *God, is everyone so dramatic around here?* Shaking my head, I turn and walk down the steps to the SUV parked at the bottom.

"I don't appreciate you contacting my friends and changing my plans. How exactly did you know they were waiting for me?" I demand when we're seated in the car.

Daniele starts the engine, his focus on the driveway as he navigates the vehicle. "We have very vigilant security and your friends are not so great at flying under the radar. Besides, Massimo told me to meet you in the lobby."

How did he even know? I stare down at my clutch, picturing the cellphone nestled inside. Has he been reading my messages? Does he know about Ethan? Is that why I can't reach him?

Questions swirl in my mind, fueling my anger toward Massimo. If he thinks he can stop me from living my life, he has another thing coming.

Chapter 16

Margot

The bass from the music vibrates through the floor and sweat permeates the air, making my head spin. I've been at Aces for four hours, I've danced with Cece and Reagan, and drank what feels like my body weight in rum. The alcohol courses through my veins, filling me with a boldness that I haven't felt since this nightmare of a marriage began.

But, if I'm being honest, it's not just the rum that fuels me. It's a culmination of things, from the sting of Ethan's message to the suffocating control that Massimo clearly thinks he has over my life. *But not tonight.* Tonight, I'm on a mission to have fun and if that includes giving *my husband* a piece of my mind, then so be it. Fueled by the conversation with my girlfriends—after disclosing how much I dislike my husband—I move along the darkened corridor.

Daniele dropped me at the entrance of Aces earlier

before heading around the back, so I don't have a clue what direction Massimo's office is in. And this might be a really bad idea that I'll regret in the morning, but... *fuck Massimo.*

Besides, if he does kill me, at least I won't be married to him anymore. I chuckle at the thought, propping myself against the wall of the corridor and drawing looks from people who pass by.

"If my husband kills me, that's got to count for something, right?" I slur to the woman heading back to the main room of the club. She cringes, her eyes wide with a look of disgust.

"It does," I mutter to myself as I move further down the corridor. "She just doesn't know the full story."

I don't realize I've reached a door until it's too late and I'm falling through it. Catching myself on the cold, metal banister a few feet inside, I narrow my eyes under the harsh glaring lights.

At the top of the staircase is a door, and with my focus on it, I lift my feet, taking the steps one at a time. *Upstairs must mean offices, right?* Yes. It's got to be this way.

I'm less than four steps up when I misjudge my footing and fall forward. As I stare at the gleaming silver metal in front of me, I can't help but release a giggle, the alcohol and giddiness of what I'm about to do lowering my inhibitions.

Crawling up the stairs on my hands and knees, I use the banister to pull myself upright when I reach the top.

Maybe I should have asked one of the girls to come with me. No, they don't need to see this.

I dust off my skirt and push through the door into a darkened corridor. It reminds me of the one in *The Shining*: impossibly endless and hiding dark secrets. I look left and then right before picking a direction and heading in search of Massimo.

Here's hoping the only psychotic person here is my husband.

Husband.

How is this my life?

Right, because *my husband* is also the reason I'm drunk on a fucking Tuesday and ready to give him a piece of my mind about his involvement in the destruction of my life.

Coming to a stop in the middle of the corridor, I tip my head back as I let my frustration, hurt, and fury flow through my body. My eyes sting with the tears I refuse to let fall; neither man deserves them.

When I bring my head back down, my eyes land on the door at the end of the corridor and the plaque that reads 'PRIVATE' in the center of it. If I were a betting woman—which I most definitely am not—I would guess that's where his office is.

Kicking off my heels, I bend to pick them up, bracing my hand against the wall when a wave of dizziness washes through me as I straighten. When I'm certain I won't pass out, I march down the hallway. I ignore the queasy feeling in the pit of my stomach, on a mission and refusing to be side-tracked.

I barrel through the door but come up short when my gaze meets that of a man cradling a gun at the end of another corridor. My pulse stutters, a weight settling on my chest before I take a cautious step forward.

"Can I help you, Mrs. Marino?"

He knows who I am. *Thank God*. This'll be easier than I thought.

"I need to see Massimo." I lift my chin, my tone defiant as I close the distance between us.

Jerking his chin, he reaches for a radio on his hip. My hand darts out before he can press the button, gripping his bicep. His gaze drops to my hand before meeting my eyes, but I don't miss the way he tenses and his eyes widen a fraction.

Releasing him, I flutter my eyelashes and lean in close. "I kinda wanna surprise him, ya know?" I pout, pushing out my chest and raising a brow.

His mouth forms an 'O' before he catches himself and scowls. For a second, I think he's going to send me on my way, but then he sighs and holds the door open. "It's the one at the end of the corridor."

Jeez, how many hallways can one place have?

Without a word, I slip through, forcing my body to relax when I hear the door close behind me. I don't give myself a second to think, barging into Massimo's office without a care in the world.

All eyes turn to me, along with the weapons of

various men dotted around the room. Massimo sits at a table, poker chips and cards strewn across the velvet. I open my mouth to speak but nothing comes out.

"Put your guns down or you won't make it out of this room alive," he commands, his eyes still on the cards in his hand.

Weapons lower, but the stares don't leave me. The quiet is thick as everyone waits for me to speak.

"What do you want, Margot?" Massimo asks, his voice cool and controlled.

It's all I need to sober myself up and remind me of my pain, anger, and circumstances that this man has caused without a thought for what he has done to me.

I step forward, the corner of my mouth lifting in a snarl. "I hate you," I snap, stamping my foot to emphasize my point. When he doesn't respond, I brave another step and then another until I'm standing in the middle of the room. "I loathe you and—"

Massimo bolts upright, and I snap my mouth shut. His eyes are on me, a storm gathering beneath the surface. He closes the distance between us in a few strides, and I expect him to stop in front of me. But he takes hold of my bicep and drags me across the room and through a door I hadn't noticed when I entered. We're in a narrow corridor and at the end it spreads out into a room, but I can't make out what the room is.

My shoes slip from my hand, landing with a thud on the hardwood floor. "Let go of me," I hiss, struggling in his hold as I try and fail to force him to release me.

In the confines of the space, Massimo turns on me, grabbing my arms and pinning them above my head against the wall. He crowds in on me until he's all I can see.

With his heat emanating over me, it's hard to think straight, the scent of whiskey and cigars surrounding me in an intoxicating haze. My lips part as I stare at him. His eyes darken, and when he presses his hips into my stomach, I feel his unmistakable hardness.

Massimo dips his head, and for a moment, I think he's going to capture my lips, but he diverts, dusting kisses along my jawline. It hasn't escaped my attention that we haven't kissed since our wedding day. But when he's licking and nipping at my skin, it's hard to concentrate and ask him why. Instead, I tilt my head to give him better access and bite down on my bottom lip to keep from moaning, conscious of the ears on the other side of the door.

Every nerve ending in my body comes alive, craving his touch. His hands release me, coming to rest on my waist, the tips of his fingers brushing over the exposed skin through the cutouts in the fabric. *It's intoxicating.* I hate how much I want this—how much I want *him*. But being this close to him, his mouth on me, the anticipation of what's to come thrumming through my veins: it's consuming.

Massimo's lips dust the shell of my ear and he murmurs, "I never would have let you leave the house in this if I'd seen you with my own eyes."

Blood rushes in my ears as I drown in his possessiveness. "You can't control what I wear," I reply breathlessly, my voice laced with an edge of neediness and defiance.

Dropping a hand to my thigh, Massimo smoothes it up the bare skin and under the slit on my right side. When he reaches my hip, he groans before dragging his hand over to my exposed pussy and growling in a possessive and downright maddening way. He hovers just above where I need him most, and a whimper slips free, my hips grinding the air as I seek out more.

He chuckles, the sound dark and depraved in the small space. "If you want something, Margot, then take it."

I don't miss the irony, but with the alcohol in my veins giving me confidence, it's all the encouragement I need. With my eyes closed in concentration, I reach for his belt buckle, unfastening it before fumbling with undoing his pants. Desperation makes my movements jerky and uncoordinated. My nipples scrape the fabric of my dress with every breath I take, only adding to my heightened arousal.

"Eyes open." Gripping my chin, Massimo forces my head back, it's only then that I open my eyes, blinking as I adjust to the dim lighting. My focus shifts to his mouth, watching as his lips move and form words. "Any time I'm going to fuck you, you look at me, Margot. You keep your eyes open and on *me*. You *think* only about me. Understood?"

I swallow the saliva that's pooled in my mouth at his

command. My hips lift toward him of their own volition, but words won't form, so I simply jerk my head in reply.

"Good girl. Now take my dick out and show me what this pretty little mouth of yours can do." He runs his thumb over my cupid's bow, before holding my chin between his finger and thumb.

I hesitate for a moment, my eyes searching his before I fall to my knees. He rubs his thumb over the apple of my cheek, his eyes hooded and heavy with lust. "You look so fucking beautiful on your knees for me."

The praise sends a rush of moisture between my legs, and I reach for his waistband, pulling his underwear and slacks down, hungry for a taste of him. His thick length is heavy and juts out less than an inch from my mouth, and I dart my tongue out, wetting my lips.

Tentatively, I wrap my hand around his length, reveling in the tortured hiss that leaves him. He's hot to the touch and impossibly hard. Lifting his length, I run my tongue from the base of his cock to the tip, swirling it around before sucking him into my mouth with my eyes trained on his face.

"Fuuucccccckkkk," Massimo groans, tipping his head back.

He dives his fingers into my hair, painfully pulling on the strands as he pushes deeper into my throat. I choke on him, saliva spluttering from my lips and running down my chin as he fills my mouth, blocking my airway.

It feels like an eternity before he pulls out, and I can breathe. Sucking in rasping breaths, I stare at him as he towers above me, stroking his cock like a goddamn god. His features are both soft and hard in the midst of his arousal, like he is willing to surrender to me or face me in a battle. *It's bewitching.*

Holding his cock at the base, Massimo uses the tip to wipe the saliva from my chin before bringing it to my open, waiting mouth. He pushes forward again, hitting the back of my throat before pulsing his hips and withdrawing. Repeating the action, he fucks my mouth like I'm his own personal sex toy. I guess, in some way, as his *unwilling* wife, I am.

My fingers inch toward my core, seeking to relieve the ache that burns there, if only for a moment. The taste of his salty pre-cum is addictive on my tongue and his musky scent fills my nostrils. This isn't my first blow job, but I never thought I'd be this turned on giving one. If anything, it's pushing me closer and closer to my orgasm than anything ever has before.

Heat coils low in my stomach, tightening with every flicker of my tongue over Massimo's cock. My hunger for him drives me, blurring my thoughts and making it hard to think beyond bringing him to completion. I convulse as I rub my fingers over the bundle of nerves at the apex of my thighs. My eyes flutter closed and pleasure spreads like liquid fire through my body.

"Your mouth feels so good, but I'm not coming down your throat tonight. Stand and face the wall," he grits through clenched teeth, sounding as close to the edge of the sweetest oblivion as I am.

I do as he commands, my need to have him filling me greater than my desire to fight. Moving my dress to the side, Massimo eases inside. My body contracts, pulling him further in, and I press my cheek into the cool wall as I moan his name.

He pulls my hair over my shoulder, his lips at my ear as he murmurs, "Now tell me how much you hate me."

I twist my head, seeking him out, searching for *something*, but when I open my mouth to speak, he pulls virtually all the way out, slamming back into me and knocking the air from my lungs.

"Don't ever come into my office and speak to me like that again. You're lucky I'm fucking you and not killing you."

He grazes his teeth over my bare shoulder, pulling out of me slowly. My walls flutter and squeeze, greedy for him to return. When he slides back in, I moan, contracting around him in a sinful and pulsating rhythm. The sounds of him filling my sex with his cock in steady thrusts mingles with our labored breaths.

"Next time, I won't hesitate to remind you of exactly who I am, and I can guarantee you won't enjoy it half as much as you're enjoying this."

His words penetrate the haze of my arousal, tinging whatever this was with ugliness. Massimo pulls out and slams into me, his movements punishing. My hands curl into fists against the wall and although I feel the pain as he repeats the action, I do nothing to stop him. Instead, I revel in his frustration, feeding on it as he pounds into me. Our labored breaths and the sound of us fucking are the only noises I can hear over the beating of my rapid pulse in my ear. Even with his harsh words hanging between us, my body is winding tighter and tighter, dragging me toward my release.

"Fuck you, Massimo," I rasp, my fury fighting with my arousal for control but losing. My eyes flutter closed, a familiar sensation as he hits my G-spot with every thrust rushing through me. Black spots appear in my vision and Massimo's fingers flex into the flesh at my hips as he holds me still.

"You can hate me all you want, Margot," Massimo murmurs low and rough, his breath hot against my ear as his thrusts grow sharper, rougher. "But your body doesn't lie. It's clear in the way your pussy sucks me in with every thrust. *You're mine.* No one else will ever touch you or have you. *Remember that.*"

I claw at the wall, desperate for my release even as it barrels through me like a freight train. A delicious shudder runs through me, and my body convulses around him before he stills, spilling inside of me.

"*Mine,*" he growls.

Seconds later, he pulls out, leaving behind an emptiness as our combined release leaks from me, coating my thighs. I can hear him dress, but I squeeze my eyes closed and drop my head until my forehead is pressed against the wall and my hair forms a curtain around me.

I hate him.

I hate the way his words wrap around me like chains,

reminding me there is no escape. But he's also right. My body craves more of him, even as my mind screams at me to run.

This was a mistake.

Not just having unprotected sex with him, but coming here, marching up to his office, and saying what I said. It was all a stupid mistake and one I don't think I'm done paying for, especially if the guilt I feel is anything to go by.

Chapter 17

Margot

Feeling sorry for myself, I burrow further into the couch, only half listening to the TV as it plays in the background. I'm nursing a killer hangover and trying to process a whole host of regrets about letting my husband fuck me against a wall in his club. Thankfully, he was gone when I woke up this morning so I was spared the embarrassment of having to face him in the cold light of day.

Unfortunately, I was not spared the embarrassment of having to ask Maria to get the morning after pill for me or asking her to take me to my doctor's to get contraception. Thankfully, she was understanding, not bothering to hide her pleased grin, and more than happy to help me out. There was no way in hell I was asking Massimo for any of that.

Groaning, I swing my legs over the back of the big white couch, hanging my head off the edge and covering my eyes with my arm. My stomach protests at the motion, threatening to bring up its contents.

No amount of carbs at breakfast seemed to do the trick of absorbing the stupid amount of alcohol I drank. I never should have returned to Cece and Reagan, or got blackout drunk hoping to wipe my memory of Massimo's touch from my mind.

I breathe through the nausea before focusing my mind on something other than how gross I feel. Immediately, X-rated images flash through my mind, sending a bolt of lust to my core that's quickly followed by a shower of guilt. I open my eyes, my focus darting around the room from one unfamiliar and upside down piece of furniture to the next. *He's so infuriating.* I know that he had something to do with the text I received from Ethan, but ruined my only chance at being able to confront him about it by letting him touch me.

Blood rushes to my head when I attempt to move, only making me feel worse. I'm halfway through shifting when I spot something peeking out from under a credenza on the far side of the room. It's tiny, a small corner of something, but the fact that it's hidden wipes away any other thoughts and forces my attention to it.

As quickly as my body will allow me, I right myself on the couch before standing. With a glance behind me to make sure the door is closed, I cross the room and grip the edges of the unit. It's heavier than I expected and I have to put my weight on my heels to push it away from the wall. It scrapes across the floor, the sound so loud that I flinch, certain that someone will have heard it.

Urgency fuels me, the fear of what will happen should I be caught snooping following quickly on my heels. My shallow breaths seem amplified in the quiet of the room and when I hear a noise somewhere in the house, I whip my head toward the door. I wait, listening intently, and when I hear nothing further, I look down the small gap I've created between the wall and the unit.

My brow furrows at what I find. Half hanging onto the back of the credenza by a single strip of tape on its corner is a thick A5 envelope. Why would Massimo keep an envelope taped to the back of a unit? Surely, he'd have a safe here or even in the club?

Carefully peeling away the tape, I take the envelope before moving the credenza back into place. I turn the envelope over as I walk back to the couch. There's no writing on the front so I think it's safe to assume it didn't come in the mail.

I slide my finger under the seal and tilt my head when I realize it hasn't been secured. Why would you go to such lengths to hide something but not seal it? Unless whoever left it behind has been returning to it regularly. That would explain the tape half hanging off.

Hesitating for a moment, I stare at the envelope. It suddenly feels heavy as if it's gained the weight of the world in the moments since I picked it up. If I uncover something I shouldn't, will they kill me? *Probably*. But

I'm married to the man who would give the order, and I don't think he would.

No. If me storming into his office and shouting at him in front of people doesn't get me killed, then finding an envelope of whatever this is, won't either.

I roll my lips together, tentatively peeking inside and assessing a wad of papers that have been haphazardly stuffed in. When I pull them out a USB stick lands on my chest with a soft thud. I stare at it, like it's a foreign object that's alien to me before picking it up and turning it over. There's nothing remarkable about it so I drop it back into the envelope and turn my attention to the papers.

I unfold them, smoothing out the crease down the center, ignoring the headache looming at the back of my head as I start pouring over the contents. *Phone records?* Sections are highlighted but none of the numbers are the same. My gaze lingers on the scrawled notes, trying to decipher the illegible handwriting. Somebody was in a hurry, that much is clear, but why?

Flipping through a couple of the pages, I find newspaper clippings with letters cut out and sheets of plain paper. *What the hell is this?* My mind instantly goes to the old school ransom notes before I dismiss the idea. Why would someone go to the effort of cutting out letters when you can create a fake email? *None of this makes any sense.*

Anxiety forms like a ball at the base of my throat. Whatever this is, it's dangerous, too dangerous to keep to myself, that much I know. I shove the papers back into the envelope along with the USB and stand. *I need to tell Massimo what I've found.*

Chapter 18

Massimo

I can still feel Margot's pussy wrapped around my cock nearly eighteen hours later. She was so fucking wet, covering me in her juices as her greedy pussy begged for more. My mind replays it like my own personal cinematic movie. The way she barreled through the door of my office, spitting her hate at me. It infuriated me but I was harder than I've ever been.

She seems to enjoy testing my patience at every turn and yet, when I'm buried deep inside of her, it feels like we've found harmony. There can be peace between us, even as I make idle threats toward her. That's why, it can't happen again. She's a distraction and distractions can only lead to consequences.

"If that's okay with you, I'll get right on it?" Daniele asks, too good at his job to ever question why I've not said a word for at least ten minutes as he's updated me on his search for Anastasia.

I move the mouse on my screen, waking it up. A grainy black and white image fills it—the moment my wife was on her knees for *me*. Tapping a few keys, I delete the footage from the server and remove all copies of the files. I meant it when I said nobody else would have her, and that includes watching her as she commits intimate acts. Besides, I'll always have the experience of her and my own personal gallery in my mind, even if I never touch her again because she's etched into me. *Fuck.* She's a vivid and untarnished memory that I couldn't erase even if I wanted to.

Closing out of the CCTV software, I pull up a shipment order, before returning my attention to Daniele. "I trust your judgment, Daniele, and I know that Romeo would too. Do whatever you have to do to bring Aurora justice."

He goes to stand when a knock sounds at the door. I have the words to enter forming on the tip of my tongue before it swings open and Margot appears on the threshold. Her eyes are wide and a little wild, like she's uncovered a truth that has the power to haunt her. But with her face free of makeup and her red hair piled on top of her head, her beauty still shines through.

"Come in, why don't you," I bite, annoyed with myself for my appraisal of her.

As if on cue, she rolls her eyes and steps inside, kicking the door closed behind her. She marches across the room, throwing an envelope onto the polished wood of my desk. It skids across the surface, only coming to a stop when I slam my hand down on top of it.

She juts her chin toward it and says, "I can just take that and leave if you'd prefer. Pretend that I didn't find anything."

I hold it up, turning it over in my hands before lifting my focus to her and raising a brow. "What is it?"

Folding her arms over her chest, she juts out her hip and huffs, "If I knew that, I wouldn't be in here."

Shaking my head, I sit forward, exasperated with her attitude. "Okay, where did you find it?"

She licks her lips, drawing my focus to her mouth and conjuring thoughts that have no place in my mind at this moment.

"In the living room behind a credenza." There's a spark of fear in her green depths, but I can't pinpoint if it's because of what she's found or how she thinks I might react.

I turn my attention to the envelope and lift the flap, emptying the contents onto the tabletop. I reach for the USB stick at the same time as Daniele reaches for the papers that have landed closer to him than me.

Turning the small stick over in my hands, I consider plugging it into my laptop before dismissing the idea. I'll get Callum to deal with it; I don't want to risk them having loaded on some sort of encryption that I'd have no idea how to undo before it could be wiped.

Placing it on my desk, I shift my focus to Daniele. "Anything of interest?"

He shuffles the papers, his brows reaching for his hairline with every page that he reads. "I'd say so. These look like the original phone records but with notes detailing where to doctor them, starting from when Rome brought Aurora here."

Shit.

My heartbeat stutters before slamming into overdrive. Excitement, anticipation and disbelief swirl inside of me like a perfect storm. *No fucking way.* I fight to convey a cool, calm and collected image, even if it couldn't be further from the truth. *My wife* has found key evidence in the search for the traitor in my home and despite how much she clearly dislikes me, she brought it to *me.* The notion makes a sense of pride flourish in my chest.

Handing the documents over and pulling me back into focus, Daniele asks, "Do you recognize the writing?"

I study the rushed and harsh writing, scouring my mind for anyone that I can recall having a similar style but in truth, we don't tend to handwrite things anymore. Sighing heavily, I come up empty, my disappointment crashing into me with the power of a wave.

The room falls quiet as the magnitude of what Margot has found sinks in.

"Is anyone going to fill me in?" Margot asks, exasperated.

Exhaling, I indicate to the empty chair across from me. "Take a seat."

She stares at me for a moment, her uncertainty

clear before she drops into the chair. Because of who she is and the position she now has in this household, Margot deserves to know the truth of what we are facing. I can't have her trying to sneak out like she did last night, especially when danger is lurking around every corner.

I rest my elbow on the arm of the chair, leaning my chin on my fist as I try to figure out where to start. "A couple of months ago, there was a targeted attack on my men. I won't get into the details, but someone has been trying to take us out ever since. In the space of two weeks, we were attacked three times and lost at least a dozen men. Things escalated when Romeo, my cousin, came over from Italy to help us in trying to figure out who was behind it."

Margot narrows her eyes. "Okay, and how does his fiancée, Aurora, factor into that? If the records are doctored from when she was here, I assume she does have *something* to do with this?"

Scrubbing a hand down my face, I shift in my seat uncomfortably. I'm not proud of how things played out with Aurora, but we did what we thought was right.

Clearing my throat, I reply, "We suspected Aurora's father of being behind the attacks. He'd worked for our family before retiring and his signature was left on one of the devices used to blow up the docks where we had a shipment coming in. We didn't know where he was and figured our best bet was to use Aurora to draw him out. Romeo ended up taking her."

"*Oh my God,*" Margot mutters under her breath, before saying louder, "You kidnapped her?"

I crack my neck. "It is how things work for us, Margot. Besides, we didn't hurt her."

"Right, because that makes taking someone against their will absolutely fine." She rolls her eyes. "I suppose I should be grateful."

"Do you want to know what's happened or are you going to keep giving me attitude?" I grind out, leaning forward before adding, "Because we both know what I told you would happen if you did that again."

There's a flicker of something heated in her gaze as she remembers last night, before she shuts it down and scoffs, pulling her finger and thumb across her lips and twisting them. She throws away an imaginary key and then glares at me.

I might just punish her anyway.

My thumb rubs over the bare skin of my ring finger, and Margot's eyes drop to the action, her nostrils flaring slightly. I don't like the restrictive feel of my wedding band on my finger so I only wear it in certain company, but it appears *that* pisses my wife off. *Interesting.*

I close my laptop and rest my arms on the cool surface. "A relationship formed between Aurora and Romeo, and a couple of weeks after we'd taken her, she received a note, instructing her to meet them in Central Park, telling her that he would be killed if she told him about it. But it was a trap. She was taken and tortured by her uncle. He made a demand of us, but by this time, someone in my ranks had fed us false information, and regrettably, we believed that Aurora was complicit. At least until Daniele uncovered information that proved otherwise."

"What happened to her uncle?" Margot rasps.

"Aurora killed him when we rescued her." I hesitate for a moment, unsure of whether it is for the best to tell her the rest before rolling my lips together and continuing, "Before she did, he confirmed that somebody in my house was plotting against me."

"Have you found them?" Uncertainty coats her words.

"No. But we are investigating, and while we do, we're keeping our circle small with only Daniele, Leonardo, Aldo, Romeo, myself, and now you, being aware of what is happening."

Bolting out of the chair, Margot slams her hands to the desk and leans closer to me. "I can't believe you. Did you not think that it would be a good idea to clue me into the fact that someone in your *own house*," her eyes widen to emphasize her point, "has been plotting to kill you and just about everyone around you?"

Running my tongue over my top teeth, I bite out, "You are on a need-to-know basis and you did not need to know."

"I beg to differ. I. Am. Your. *Wife*. That entitles me to know whatever the hell you know. Especially when I could be the one they come after next."

"Margot," I growl, the warning clear in my tone.

She holds up a hand. "No. You can't do that. You don't get to tell me off for being pissed at you for this. You're in the wrong whether you admit it or not." She shakes her head, scoffing before she heads for the door. "I'm going to have a nap, don't wake me up unless you're going to apologize. I've had enough of you today."

The door closes with a soft click behind her.

"I like her." Daniele chuckles, filling the silence.

His laughter dies down when I level him with a hard stare and sneer. "Don't you have something you should be doing?"

He smirks, standing and picking up the USB stick. "I'll get Callum to check this out."

I'm too busy thinking over what Margot said. I should have made sure she was aware of the dangers surrounding her. *She's right*. The words taste bitter and yet I haven't spoken them aloud. I'm not sure I ever will.

Even if she is right, it doesn't mean she can get away with speaking to me like that. Margot needs to learn her place in my life, and I will have no problem showing her when she least expects it.

There's only so much leeway I can give her and what with her antics so far—contacting her ex, sneaking out and storming into my office—I'm close to snapping.

Chapter 19

Margot

Massimo strides into the kitchen when I'm halfway through my breakfast. I didn't see him again yesterday after he told me what had happened to Aurora and the attacks on him and his men. He should have told me sooner, preferably before we got married, instead of blindly bringing me into his life.

In some ways, I'm grateful that I didn't see him again because I was so mad and I definitely would have pushed him further. I probably would have made demands I didn't mean, like wanting to know who they suspected and then we'd have fought more at his unwillingness to tell me.

I feel his presence as he heads for the table, but I don't acknowledge him. He sets down a plate of eggs and a cup of espresso before sliding into his chair. The tension around us is almost suffocating, but I refuse to break the silence.

Only the sound of cutlery scraping across china fills the room and when Massimo finishes his plate, he uses his napkin to wipe his mouth. He stands, rolling up the sleeves of his shirt. My gaze is fixed on his corded, thick forearms, watching his every move. A needy ache forms in my gut, and I bite back the whimper that nearly slips from my lips when he picks up my plate and clears the table.

"Hey, I wasn't finished," I protest, turning in my chair.

He places the plates on the countertop, quietly saying something to Alma. She darts a concerned glance over at me before lifting her gaze back to Massimo and dipping her chin. My mind races and I try to understand the scene unfolding in front of me as she scurries from the room.

I turn my attention back to Massimo and find him cracking his neck, eyes fixed on the ceiling before he shifts his focus to me. Panic flares in my chest as I notice the intent in his gaze. I stand, moving around the table as he stalks toward me.

"You can't escape this, Margot." There's a thread of something in his tone that weaves a web of trepidation up my spine.

This is it.

How ridiculous that I'm going to die because I couldn't control my annoyance. *Again*. Dread unfurls inside of me, sinking deep into my bones and colliding with the panic at what is to come. I should have known I wouldn't get away with what happened at the club so easily.

I hold up my hand as he moves closer, before inching away and trying to keep a distance between us. "You don't have to do this," I plead, my breath shaking with every inhale.

"That's where you're wrong." He pauses, his steps slow and deliberate. "You've left me with no choice." Another beat of silence as fear and excitement pulse through my body. "I warned you and you chose to ignore me." His tone is low and laced with an edge of warning. "Clearly, I need to follow through with actions to ensure you don't make the same mistake again."

I stumble over a chair, knocking it into the table, the sound loud in the otherwise quiet room. Massimo uses my momentary distraction as I attempt to steady myself to his advantage, banding his arms around me and pulling my body flush against his. The air is knocked from my lungs at the sudden movement before I sink into the heat of his body, with my back pressed to his front.

Instinctively, I relax into him before I catch myself and stiffen. *I refuse to make this easy for him.* My fingers scratch at his arm, trying to pry myself out of his hold as I wriggle against him.

Unfazed, he dusts his nose up the exposed column of my throat and I curse myself for having tied my hair up. I swallow thickly and close my eyes, trying and failing to fight against my arousal. It's hard, especially when it's so consuming. His teeth graze my earlobe, the brief jolt of pain sending a bolt of lust to my core.

"Hands on the table," he grates.

I lean away from him, my question hanging between us. When he doesn't speak, I do as he demands, slowly resting my hands on the wooden surface and bending at the waist, even as my mind screams at me to run.

Massimo steps behind me, one hand on the center of my back and the other on my hip. I feel his power without him needing to speak and the anticipation of what's to come sends a rush of wetness between my legs. He steps closer until I can feel his hard cock, pressing against my ass.

He's a monster.

I wonder if he can feel the heat of my pussy through the fabric of my dress. *Is he turned on by the thought of whatever he's about to do?*

I want to lash out and call him sick for getting turned on by hurting me, but that would make me a hypocrite and I can't trust my voice not to give me away. Yet I'm so turned on by him that I fear I'm addicted, that only *he* will be able to make me feel this way. *And what does that say about me?*

"You've defied me four times, Margot." Smoothing a hand over my ass, Massimo lifts my dress, exposing me to him. "That's four punishments," he murmurs distractedly.

I wait for him to move, anticipation replacing the uncertainty.

"If you thought I wouldn't punish you for your little outburst yesterday or all the things you have done since you became mine, then you don't know me at all. Actions have consequences, Margot. These are yours."

I'm too caught up in my shock to fully process what he's saying. He draws his hand back and I tense, bracing myself on the table.

The first thwack of his hand on my ass cheek sends me jolting forward and crying out at the unexpected pain that shoots through me and leaves my skin tingling. "One," he counts, his voice controlled and smooth.

I try to move, to turn away from him and protect myself before the next assault comes but he holds me still, his power no match for me. His hand lands in the same place, the intensity still there, but the pain that follows quickly morphs into pleasure.

"Two."

My fingers claw at the wood beneath me and a low growl vibrates in my chest. *I hate him.* The next two slaps come in quick succession, but both equally as painful as the last, as he counts each one of them like he's committing them to memory. Shame prickles under my skin, mingling with a dangerous heat that is impossible to ignore as moisture pools between my legs. Once again, my body is betraying me in a fight I've already lost.

Heat fills my chest, the cool surface beneath doing nothing to ease it. I bite down on the inside of my cheek to keep from moaning, refusing to give him the satisfaction of hearing how much his 'punishment' is actually my pleasure.

Massimo rubs his hand over the spot where he's hit me. I know it's got to be hot to the touch because his palm is cool and soothing. When he presses his hip against my other cheek, I feel his hardness again.

His fingers graze my bare flesh as he straightens my skirt. There's a gentleness to his movements, but it's almost mocking. Without a second glance, he steps away, returning to his seat and picking up his espresso cup. "What do you have planned for today?"

I straighten, my eyes widening as I look around the room. *What the fuck?* The sting of his hand lingers on my skin, but it's the casual note to his voice that throws me. I've got whiplash from how quickly he's shifted gears. My heart still beats an erratic rhythm in my chest as I stare at him, trying to figure out what has just happened. *Is this his idea of normal?*

"Nothing. I—" My mind is completely gone, the delicious ache spreading through my body all I can focus on. I shouldn't be turned on by what he's done, I should be angry and demanding an apology. But all I can think about is the release my body is craving. *What the hell is happening?*

Standing, Massimo takes his wallet out of his slacks. He pulls a black card from the folds, chucking it down on the table. "Why don't you get out of the house and do some shopping? I'll have someone waiting for you in the entryway in an hour."

Then, he strides from the kitchen, leaving me to deal with the aftermath of whatever the hell *that* was.

With my skin still burning from his touch and my mind reeling with a cocktail of anger and desire, I stare at the black card. Its presence is a reminder of the control Massimo continues to have over me.

Will I ever be free?

Chapter 20

Margot

Enraged, I march through the house. I'm on a mission, one man on my mind with a thousand questions that demand answers.

With everything I know about Massimo and the danger that fills his world, it shouldn't have surprised me that he would have sent me shopping with two people, only to have another follow us from the shadows. He should have told me that was his plan.

I thought I'd made myself clear.

He keeps me in the loop and I don't lose my shit at him.

I'm reminded of the events in the kitchen this morning. Of him punishing me for speaking my mind in front of others. But maybe he was sending a different message, reminding me of who is in charge in our relationship.

Well, he's going to get a piece of my mind now. I don't care who he's in his office with. He should have given me a heads-up. It's the least he can do given everything. I'm not used to watching over my shoulder and reasoning with my paranoia when I see a shifty as fuck man obviously following me.

I barge into Massimo's office, balling my hands. I inhale sharply before blowing it out and marching across the room. *Thank God he's alone.* The hour and a half drive from the city was more than enough time for the ire to seep into my bones and rid me of any manners.

"Margot," Massimo drawls, a bored note to his tone as he continues to type on his laptop.

With my hands on my hips, I step into the room, kicking the door shut behind me. "I know I'm not from your world, Massimo, and Lord knows everyone likes to remind me of the fact. But can you please explain why you sent two people to the city with me and then had someone else following us the entire time?" My chest heaves, but I bite my tongue, holding back, waiting for him to explain himself.

He lifts his head, focusing his attention on me. "You clearly have more to say, so get it all out, because this will be your only chance."

He's barely finished his sentence before I speak again. "What was the point? Other than to freak me out." Pacing, I throw my hands up in the air. "Do you not think it might have been a good idea to tell me? Of course you didn't. Why should you tell me anything? Honestly, Massimo, I thought I'd been clear about this. You can't leave me out of the loop on these things. I need to know if I should have my guard up when—"

I snap my mouth shut, my heart thumping in my chest when I turn and watch Massimo roll his chair back. He closes his laptop, moving it to the side and taps the mahogany desk. "Come. Sit."

Torn between running and following my curiosity, I remain rooted to the spot. There isn't a chance in hell that I'm going to willingly let him spank me again. "No," I affirm, jutting my chin. "I'm not a dog you can beckon, and I'm sure as hell not up for another round of your twisted discipline when I've done nothing wrong."

His expression darkens. "Margot," he rumbles. "Sit, before I make you."

My heart thrashes, and a heavy silence settles between us until the tension snaps in the air. Unable to stand the weight of his stare any longer, I tear my gaze away, walking around his desk with stiff and deliberate steps. I hesitate before lifting myself onto the cool wood. The polished surface sticks to the backs of my thighs before Massimo rolls his chair in and lifts my legs, resting my feet on the arms of it.

He holds me steady when I go to move, gripping my ankles firmly. The cocktail of excitement and apprehension swirling inside of me is too much to bear. "Look, I'm..." I huff out a breath, turning to look out of the window at the vibrant and dewy landscape. "I'm sorry, okay? I shouldn't have barged in here—"

My hips lift, and a gasp is ripped from my lips when

he applies a light pressure to my clit over my panties. I stare at him through hazy eyes before my head rolls back, suddenly too heavy. *I'm supposed to be mad at him.* I should be shoving him away and reminding him of why I stormed in here, but when I look at him again, the heat in his eyes locks me in place. The corner of his mouth lifts and my body practically sings in anticipation of the release that I know only he can give me.

"You *can* apologize. That's good to know." Running his hands up my legs and under my skirt, he grips my underwear, pulling them down my thighs when I lift from the desk. "I have no problem filling you in on matters, Margot. But you need to remember that it's not all sunshine and roses. If you can't handle something, there's no giving it back."

I nod, my resolve faltering as a sliver of unease skates down my spine. "I know."

Bringing my legs together in front of him, Massimo finishes removing my underwear. I expect him to throw them on the floor or put them on the desk, but instead, he opens his desk drawer, dropping them inside. When he closes it, the sound lingers in the air, heightening my need to feel his hands on me.

I lean back, resting my hands on the desk behind me when he returns his hands to my thighs, smoothing up the inside of them and massaging the flesh with his fingers. My eyes flutter closed when he swipes his thumb over my clit. I gasp at the sensation, the bundle of nerves sensitive to the touch.

Suddenly he's gone, and I open my eyes, seeking him out.

"It's polite to look someone in the eye when you're having a conversation," he admonishes.

I lick my lips and clear my throat before shuffling on the desk and holding his gaze. "Of course."

My chest heaves, all of my concentration going into holding Massimo's stare as he slides a finger inside of me. I whimper, my hips rocking forward when he doesn't move.

"I didn't send anyone to follow you."

A whirlwind of worry picks up in my gut, but with a light pressure to my clit and the movement of his finger, Massimo calms it.

"Who was it then?" I ask, my words breathless and laced with arousal.

He adds another finger, muttering under his breath, "You're so fucking wet." Sitting straighter, he adds, "I don't know. I sent you with Angelo and Dante, that was all. But rest assured, I will find out who was following you."

Applying more pressure to my clit, he works his thumb in small circles, bringing me closer to the edge. "Okay," I sigh, my mind too focused on the movements of his hand to fully process his words.

"What do you remember about him?" Massimo asks, completely unfazed.

Oh God. I can barely remember my own name when he has his hands on me. Scouring my memory, I try to recall the guy I'd seen as we traveled from store to store. It was busy but he stood out.

Massimo pushes my skirt further up my legs, exposing my pussy. He lowers his head between my thighs and blows a stream of cold air onto it. I moan at the sensation that follows. "Keep thinking. This is important."

Right. Yes. Important. What did he look like? I stare at the wall behind Massimo, trying and failing to remember. When his tongue slides through my folds, I give up; a moaned gasp falling from my lips and flying around the room. My hips lift, following his mouth when he moves away.

"Fuck, you taste good." He continues to move his fingers in and out of me at a lazy pace. "What did he look like?"

"I can't think when you're doing that," I breathe. When he removes his fingers, I cry out in frustration and pout. "No. I need more."

Massimo stands, forcing me to lift my legs from the chair as it rolls back. I fall back onto the desk, resting my heels on the edge. The sound of him undoing his belt and dragging it through the loops sends a thrill of excitement through me. He drops it to the floor, the metallic sound brash but barely penetrating the fog of arousal surrounding me.

Within seconds, his cock is free and he's gripping the base as he enters me. He's still fully clothed and there's something carnal about the vision of him with only his cock bared. I shift to sit up, staring down at where we're connected as he eases inside of me, inch by glorious inch.

Our moans collide in the space between us, his deep and masculine, mine soft and low. I slide my palm up his chest, resting it on his shoulder while keeping the other planted to the desk. I hook my legs over his hips, pulling him even closer to me.

Massimo drops his forehead against mine and we hold each other's stare as he moves in and out with agonizingly slow thrusts. The moment feels intimate and like there's a whole heap of meaning behind it that I don't have the capacity to process. Each stroke of his cock stokes the flames inside of me. I moan his name, my eyes heavy and hard to keep open.

I know that he must feel what I do, because he pulls back, slamming into me over and over again, his movements jerky and uncontrolled. Tension coils in the base of my spine, and I dig my fingers into his shoulder as I match his pace.

My back arches and my walls clamp around Massimo's cock. Rocking my hips, I cry out, tremors wracking my body as my orgasm rushes through me. Massimo grunts, dropping his head to my shoulder as he stills and comes inside of me.

When he straightens, he smooths a strand of hair away from my face, the gesture reinforcing the intimacy we shared moments ago.

The sounds of the house on the other side of his office door are suddenly amplified, like someone turned up the volume. They remind me of where we are and why I came to his office.

Pushing at his stomach, I force him to step back before jumping from his desk. I'm aware of him rearranging his clothes and tucking his cock back into his trousers.

As I move around the room, trying to put some distance between us, I feel our release sliding down my leg and curse myself for having let him steal my panties and come inside me again.

It's only when I've got my breathing under control that I dare speak, forcing myself to answer his question from earlier. "I don't remember what he looked like exactly, but he was shifty and had tattoos. If I saw him again, I'd recognize him, but he was too far away to get any real details."

Dropping into his chair, Massimo opens his laptop, dismissing me. "I'll pick up with Angelo and Dante to see if they got anything."

I take that as my cue to leave. I still feel the heat of him lingering on me as I move through the house. But what's worse is the guilt over Ethan that always follows hot on its heels.

If my husband's touch is like a brand that I don't think I'll ever be able to scrub away, then the memory of my ex-boyfriend is like a ghost that will haunt me forever.

Chapter 21

Margot

I flip the page of the book I'm reading, my mind half on the story and half on the scene beyond the window. Thick raindrops streak the glass, the remnants of the early morning downpour that left puddles across the property, and a vibrancy to the grass and trees. I snuggle further into the oversized armchair, tucking my blanket around me as a gust of wind thrashes the trees around.

Facing the window, I'm blocked from the view of anyone passing in the corridor, but I can also pretend that the world on the other side of the door doesn't exist. *Especially Massimo.* We've been cordial this past week, but there's a growing tension between us, fraught with a sexual energy that could combust at any moment.

Thankfully, neither of us has acted on it, and the time we've spent dancing around each other has helped me to firm up my resolve. Massimo is a monster, this much I know. The problem is, when we're caught up in the cloud of lust, it's hard to remember everything he's done and how he came into my life.

My mind drifts to Ethan, guilt tumbling over me like an avalanche and settling onto my chest; heavy and suffocating. I rest the book in my lap, gazing out of the window as I wait for it to pass.

At times, when Massimo is playing the strings of my body like a skilled musician, it feels like I've given in too soon. As if I waved my white flag and surrendered to my husband, when the man I really love is out in the world, waiting for me. *Is he though?* I haven't heard from Ethan since his message telling me to try and make things work with Massimo. It's like he's given up on us, and I can't really blame him for that.

Resting my head against the back of the chair, I blink back the moisture that pools in my eyes. The loss of him feels like grief, as if he'd died and I have no hope of ever seeing him again. In some ways, I think that would have made this easier, at least then I'd have nothing to hold on to.

Smoothing my hand over the worn page of the book, I blink away my sorrow and begin reading again. My finger traces the words as I read about a heroine torn from her love. I get lost in their world, pretending my story could end like theirs, where the girl gets her guy.

"I don't know what else you want me to tell you. It's

gone." A hushed male voice drowning in urgency cuts through the quiet. His low tone speaks of secrecy, but rather than tuning him out, I steady my breathing and listen intently.

I wait for him to continue, but he doesn't, the only sound in the room is that of the fire crackling beside me. Closing my book, I quietly slide it onto the coffee table, my movements slow and methodical.

"Yes, I've searched the room." He pauses, his footsteps on the plush carpet faint but an indication of his pacing. "There's no envelope, only a piece of tape."

Is he talking about the envelope I found? My breath halts as I stare at my reflection in the window. *Could this be the person Massimo told me about?* The one who has been plotting to kill him from within his own ranks?

I could confront him, burst into the corridor, and demand to know why. The idea sparks to life before my common sense can kick in but when it does, I shut the idiotic thought down. Anyone in this house is dangerous and should be approached with caution. And I am not the person to be confronting people who are trained to kill.

Right now, I'm nothing more than a shadow on the other side of the door. I should stay where I am and deny having heard anything if he comes in. *But if I move closer, I might be able to see who it is.*

Swallowing down my nerves, I ease myself out of the chair, wary of making a sound and alerting them to my presence. My breaths are short and shallow, but as I cross the room and hide myself behind the door, they sound loud and exaggerated to my own ears.

I angle my body to peek through the gap where the door meets the frame. From where he's standing—on the corner of where the corridor turns—it's impossible to see him properly. But there's a familiarity to his voice, even with the thread of panic lacing it.

From my new vantage point, I can just about hear another voice; it's loud but the words are indecipherable as they shout on the other end of the phone.

"I am very aware of what Mattia did." He pauses. "Yes, he fucked us over, but I won't let that happen again." He moves around the corridor, his voice growing distant before becoming clearer. "I think if he'd found it, I'd have been told. Stupidly, they've brought me in on the search for me." He lets out a dark, sinister chuckle that sends a shiver down my spine.

I close my eyes, trying to place his voice, to recall his face, but it's no use.

Pressing my back to the wall, I suck in a breath, covering my mouth with my hand when the mystery man moves closer to the library door and pushes it open. I daren't move, frozen in place with him on the other side of the door.

"I'll keep you updated," he murmurs distractedly. "I've got to go."

His footsteps fade as he leaves, and I don't breathe

until I'm certain that he's gone. The danger Massimo spoke of isn't just real—it's *here* and I've stumbled straight into its path. But the fear curling in my gut only makes my resolve harden. I have to figure out who he is.

Too much is depending on it.

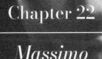

Chapter 22

Massimo

Daniele and I are in the living room reviewing a planned shipment. The door is closed, affording us some privacy while we wait for Aldo to join us. He returned this morning from a two-day stakeout at Elio Morretti's old estate in New York City.

Elio hasn't returned since we attacked his Manhattan house a few weeks back. Our men take twenty-four-hour shifts watching his place, but I'm not optimistic that he'll be back. If he knows what's good for him, he'll have left New York for good, because the moment he steps out of hiding, we'll be ready and waiting for him.

In the meantime, we need to find the rat. Every day that passes, with no indication of who it is only makes us look weak. The other families are watching our every move, waiting for us—*for me*—to slip up so they can strike and take everything my father and his father worked so hard for.

"Come in," I call in answer to the knock at the door.

Aldo enters, closing it behind him. "Apologies for my tardiness, there was something I had to take care of." He takes a seat on the couch across from me and next to Daniele.

I slide the documents I was reading onto the coffee table, resting my elbows on my parted knees. "While you were away, Margot found an envelope. It was hidden in this room with a USB drive, newspaper clippings and phone records in it. The documents look like they were the originals of the doctored ones you were given."

"Oh?" There's a flicker of something in Aldo's gaze, but it's too quick for me to fully decipher. It's enough to send a trickle of doubt down my spine.

Sitting taller, I mentally shake off the feeling and continue, "It's safe to say that somewhere between the documents being handed to you and you bringing them to my office, they were switched out. The question is, by who?"

Aldo nods in agreement. "I took a call and left the documents on the kitchen counter. They must have been watching me and took the opportunity because it couldn't have been more than five minutes before I returned."

"You're not to blame for this, Aldo," I reassure him.

Aldo has worked for my family for years. I've brought him into the fold because he's someone we can trust. *Is he?* Without a shadow of a doubt, I know he has nothing to do with this. That doubt I felt a moment ago was unwarranted; he's done *nothing* but show loyalty for decades.

Turning to Daniele, I incline my head, indicating for him to share what he's found out about the contents of the envelope. He sighs, frustration and exhaustion seeping from his body—he's a mirror of how we all feel.

"Callum had to work his magic on this one. The contents of the USB were encrypted, and it took him longer than normal to get into it. I switched off when he tried to talk me through the steps, but he confirmed it was created by the same person who hosted the live feed of Aurora being tortured by Anastasia when they made their demands."

That's something, but it's not enough for us to make any real progress, which we've been lacking ever since we found Aurora. I crack my neck to ease the tension that's been building since the start of this meeting. "Okay. That's good to know, but we've taken care of him so it doesn't move us any further forward. What I want to know is how it ended up in my house, stuck to the back of a credenza?"

Daniele shrugs, running a hand through his hair. "The simple answer? No idea. Callum's helping me scour all of the footage we have, but I'm not holding my breath that we'll find anything. This has been well thought through and whoever it is clearly has people on their side that could help with hacking into our systems and erasing recordings."

"So what *do* we have?" I snap.

"I've sent the envelope to a forensics guy Leonardo recommended. He'll look for DNA or prints, but he's backed up at work and has to fit us in without raising suspicions, so that could take some time."

Standing, I move to the bar in the corner of the room. We're nowhere new and at every turn, it feels like we're ten steps behind.

Pouring three tumblers of whiskey, I return to the couches and hand them out. "Let's figure out a way forward. There haven't been any more attacks since the warehouse, but that doesn't mean there won't be and we need to get ahead."

Aldo sips his drink before placing it on the table. "You've been at this for weeks, Daniele. It's not a question of capability, because we all know you are more than capable, but it's evident that you're exhausted. Besides, you've got your hands full with Anastasia and we can't afford to lose focus there. Let me take this off your plate."

My attention shifts to Daniele, who lifts a shoulder. Nodding, I instruct, "Daniele, I want you to keep looking for Anastasia. She can't have just disappeared into thin air. Hand over whatever you have on the rat to Aldo, and we'll reconvene at the end of the week. It goes without saying, if you get a break before then, let me know."

"Yes, boss," they reply in unison.

"Good, now that we have that sorted, has there been any luck with finding the guy that was trailing Margot?"

Daniele nods, shifting forward in his seat. "Yes,

Angelo provided a good description of the guy. We've got it circulating and I'm confident that we'll have him soon."

My relief is palpable. "Okay. If she wants to go anywhere, I want at least four men with her."

"*Capisco*," Daniele replies before continuing, "If there's nothing else..."

I wave my hand, indicating that they're free to leave.

Daniele stands, inclining his head to me before turning to Aldo. "Come, let me get my files for you and we can go over them."

They leave the living room, and I walk to the window, staring out at the gardens in front of me. It's not just my life at risk now, whoever is intent on taking down my family has their eyes set on Margot too, otherwise, why would they be following her?

I'll be damned if I let them touch her. A possessiveness takes root in my chest at the thought of her. I'm becoming far too attached to someone I married because it was convenient.

Chapter 23

Margot

The pulsating bass of the music vibrates through the air. Bodies surround me on the dance floor of Aces, pressed together and moving as one in a tantalizing and hypnotic rhythm. Strobe lights flicker, painting the scene in electric blue and white flashes.

Cece and Reagan are somewhere ahead of me and a stranger's hands grip my hips, their hold impersonal as I move to the beat of the music. With my eyes closed, I allow myself to forget everything that's happened over the last couple of weeks.

At least until something dark hovers in front of me, an unwelcome presence, forcing me to open my eyes. I don't stop dancing as I stare at the six-foot-five wall of muscle standing in front of me. Lights flash behind him, but I can still make out the scowl etched into his features. My stomach clenches at the menacing sight.

He leans forward a fraction, shouting to be heard

over the music. "Mrs. Marino, you need to come with me."

Something about the way he says it, with anger layered beneath a command, sets me on edge. My gut twists, dread and doubt swirling in my chest. Massimo might be controlling but he would never do something this public. *Wouldn't he?* The truth is, I have no idea. This could be a ploy to kidnap me, or it could be Massimo's way of getting me to leave. The reality is, I don't know enough to judge it either way.

I stare at the man in front of me, categorizing his features. A tattoo snakes around his neck, and on the left side of his top lip, there's a scar. He's wearing a polo shirt that all the employees who work for Massimo in this club wear and looped over his ear is the earpiece I've seen on the staff. It calms the sense of unease that washed through me when he first appeared.

Folding my arms over my chest, I narrow my eyes and stop dancing. Tilting my head, I reply, "If he sent you, tell him that I'm not leaving yet."

Either he doesn't hear me, or he's purposely ignoring me, because he steps back, waving his arm in front of himself. A bead of unease seeps into my stomach, but I blow out a breath, shaking it off.

Rolling my eyes, I turn away, intent on heading back to the VIP area and enjoying the rest of my night. If he won't tell Massimo, I'll make sure he gets the message myself.

A large hand wraps around my arm, pulling me back.

The abrupt movement causes my ankle to roll in my six-inch heels. My eyes widen, darting around the sea of people in front of me, searching for Reagan and Cece or *anyone*. Panic claws at my throat, and when I open my mouth to scream for help, nothing comes out.

As if I weigh nothing, the guy drags me across the dance floor, the club-goers around us continuing to party and oblivious to what is happening to me. Hell, *I* don't know what is happening to me.

We're heading for the corridor that I know leads to Massimo's office, his grip tight and painful on my arm as he marches forward, ignoring our mismatched strides.

I pull back, digging my heels in with desperation fueling me. *He's too strong.* We enter the dark corridor I walked down days ago and it doesn't escape me how different I feel now, with panic and fear clawing at my skin, than I did then.

When we reach the door that leads to the steps for the second floor, he pushes it open before shoving me across the threshold. I falter slightly, holding on to the banister just in front of me and turning to face the wall, keeping my back to him. As the door clicks shut, engulfing us in silence, he takes my arm, pulling me up the metal staircase.

"You're making a mistake," I urge, trying to reason with him. "Let me go, and we can forget this ever happened."

He scoffs, opening the door when we reach the top step. "The only one making a mistake is you. Besides, I'm not going to have it on my head that the boss's *whore of a wife* embarrassed him in his own fucking club." He sneers, pushing me across the threshold.

I fall forward, slamming into the wall ahead of me from the force. Slowly, I turn to face him, lifting my chin as I push back the hair that's fallen in front of my face. "And you think calling his wife a whore is going to do you any favors?"

His lip curls as he crowds me in, but I hold his gaze, refusing to cower. He bares his teeth in a snarl as he growls, "Who's he going to believe, the loyal soldier or the woman he took because he likes shiny things? They call him the Crow for a reason." He lifts my left hand, tilting his head as he *tsks*. "And she can't even keep her wedding rings on."

I have no retort. *He's right.* Why would Massimo take my word over that of a 'loyal' man? And my rings aren't on my finger; I shoved them into my purse on the drive here, wanting to pretend for a moment that my life was back to normal. Yanking my arm, he marches me toward the door at the end of the corridor.

"For the last time, let me go." There's no way I'm going to allow this Neanderthal to drag me to my husband like I'm some naughty child. "This is your last chance."

"Or what? You'll pull a gun out on me? Yeah, I'd like to see you try." He laughs, the sound loud and mocking.

I narrow my eyes before lifting my hand and digging my nails into his arm, dragging them along his flesh and leaving bloody scratch marks in their wake. A triumphant smirk tugs at my lips when he releases me, air hissing from his mouth, and I lift my chin, aiming it at him. *That'll teach him to fuck with me.*

His hand flies up, the sharp crack of his palm connecting with my cheek echoing in the corridor. My vision blurs as my head snaps sideways, and I slam into the wall, smacking my temple against the cold plaster. Pain explodes across my face, and I gasp for air as I struggle to stay upright. My mouth fills with a metallic taste and tears burn in my eyes.

"Stupid bitch," he snarls, taking hold of my arm and dragging me in the direction of Massimo's office.

My head swims, the pounding behind my eyes so intense it feels like a drumbeat. *Did that really just happen?* He fucking hit me. Hard. I blow out a shaky breath, blinking slowly as I try to process the interaction.

"You only have yourself to blame," he mutters, shaking his head.

When we reach the office, the door is opened by one of the men on guard. He nods to my assailant and I'm ushered inside. The man's grip doesn't waver, as if this is a normal way to treat a person. *I guess in their world, it is.*

Massimo lifts his head, his dark eyes locking onto mine, along with those of everyone else in the room. I don't know what he must see, but if the way his gaze narrows and the vein in his temple pulses is any indication, he's furious. His attention shifts to the hand on my arm and I'm certain that if he could shoot lasers from his eyes, the man would be dead.

The room tilts, the voices around me muffled as if coming from underwater. My legs buckle slightly, but the iron grip on my arm keeps me from falling.

I think I need to lie down.

Chapter 24

Massimo

Like a missile locked on its target, I can't tear my gaze away from the hand wrapped around Margot's arm. Fury seeps into my blood, turning what was once a pleasant evening into an ugly affair.

Abandoning my weekly poker game, I throw my cards onto the table and into my stack of chips, without a care for how they land, and lean back in my chair.

Exhaling, I try to calm the beast inside of me. "Release her," I bite, my words cold as ice.

The *fucker*—I don't even know his name—stares at me dumbfounded, like my demand isn't quite aligned with how he expected this conversation to go. His grip tightens, his knuckles turning white against her pale skin.

"Get. Your. Fucking. Hands. Off. My. Wife," I bellow, pushing to stand and knocking my chair to the floor.

A hush falls over the room, the attention of the other

players at the table and their security dotted around the room, shifting to us and the scene playing out. Still clutching her arm, wide eyes dip to her before lifting to meet mine. As if presenting her to me, he pushes Margot forward and under the overhead light.

There's a noticeable redness on her left cheek and right temple that I'm certain can't be blamed on alcohol. *If he's fucking touched her, I'll kill him.* When Margot lifts her glassy eyes to mine, I rest my hand on my gun, ready to make my move.

Daniele steps forward and into my peripheral. "Russo, let her go," he commands.

Russo's gaze shifts to Daniele, but he still doesn't free her. My hand moves before I can think. The weight of my gun is steady in my grip as I lift it and aim for his head.

I do something I've never done before and hesitate. There is no doubt in my mind about what I have to and want to do, but a small voice in the back of my mind tells me to hold back, for Margot's sake, to protect her from the violence. I silence it, I have to. Letting this asshole get away with manhandling her is not an option. I will make an example out of him.

Without further thought, I pull the trigger. The crack of the shot splits the air, bouncing off the walls and colliding with the thud of his body hitting the floor. He drags Margot backward momentarily before his dead body relaxes and he releases her.

She turns slightly, looking down at him, her arms

flailing as she tries to steady herself. A whimper slips free before she returns her attention to me and sets her shoulders.

When her focus drifts back to him and her chin trembles, I call, "Margot."

She snaps her eyes back to me and swallows thickly before nodding. In that moment, she looks so young; like the bravado she usually carries around has been ripped away. *That's because of me.*

Clearing my throat and ridding my mind of the unwelcome thought, I continue, "Keep your eyes on me and come here."

She sucks in a shaky breath and crosses the room. I hold my arm out, tucking her into my side when she reaches me, a sense of ease settling into me when she clutches at my shirt. *Fuck.* This isn't how I saw the evening unfolding.

I smooth my thumb over her hip, then I turn to address the room. "Gentlemen, apologies for cutting the evening short, but it's clearly for the best, given my hand. Lorenzo will get you squared away and I'll see you next week." Inclining my head to them, I step away from the table, guiding Margot in the direction of my private apartment. "Daniele?" I call over my shoulder, my request unspoken but clear.

"I've got it, boss."

Margot trembles against me as we cross the space. It doesn't escape my attention that the last time we came in here, we didn't make it past the hallway. The memory makes my cock twitch, but I ignore it, focusing on making sure Margot is okay and getting to the bottom of what the fuck has happened tonight.

As we enter the apartment, I guide her to the couch. The space is basic and nothing like the luxury of the house in Stony Brook. It consists of two rooms, a bedroom at the back and a living room with a kitchenette.

With Margot settled on the couch, I head to the cabinet where I keep a bottle of whiskey. I grab a glass, returning to her, and taking a seat on the coffee table. She stares at the same spot, spaced out and unseeing. Concern tugs at the muscle in my chest. *I don't know how to fix this.*

Pouring a drink, I hand it over, watching as she throws it back before handing the glass back. I set it on the table and pick up her hand, rubbing my finger over the spot where her wedding band should be. It rattles me more than it should to see my ring missing. "Where are your rings?"

Margot blinks, looking at her hand and then back at me before trying to pull herself free. "Let go of me."

Something in her tone makes my chest ache, and I release her, not wanting to add to her turmoil. She rubs her palms over her thighs, scanning the room before standing.

I fight the urge to comfort her, to tell her that she's safe with me because that would be a lie. *I am the reason* she is feeling how she feels now. I'm the reason she had to endure whatever that piece of shit did to her.

"Margot," I call, drawing her attention to me as she moves around the room. She glances at me over her shoulder, waiting for me to continue. "Where are your rings?"

She runs her finger over the books lining the shelf near the TV. "I took them off and put them in my purse."

I narrow my eyes, sighing heavily. "And where's your purse now?" She didn't have it when she was dragged into my office.

Facing me, she sets a hand on her hip, her top lip curling. "You are such a hypocrite. Where's your ring, Massimo? You think I haven't noticed that you don't wear it?"

Standing, I hold my hand up, showing her my wedding band before stuffing my hands into my pockets. "I'll let it slide because of what you've been through tonight, Margot. But you're wearing my patience thin. Where are your rings?"

"Always letting it slide," she mutters under her breath before moving back to the couch and flopping down. "I left it in the VIP booth."

I pull out my phone and send a text to Daniele, telling him to pick it up.

Turning toward me with teary eyes, Margot asks, "You didn't think to let it slide with him?" A cocktail of fear and something akin to hurt swirls in her gaze, and for a split second, I'm not sure how to respond.

I move to the couch, reaching for her and pulling her onto my lap. She straddles me, and I tilt my head back, moving my thumbs in small circles on the bare skin of her thighs. "What happened with him?"

Margot huffs out a breath, wrapping her arms around herself. "Do you want me to work backward from the part where you shot a man or should I end there?"

Running my tongue over my teeth, I remind myself of what she's endured tonight. "Start from when he approached you."

She looks away, rolling her lips together before meeting my stare again. "I was dancing. He came over, told me I had to go with him. I said no. He brought me upstairs anyway, and then you shot him."

Fuck, she's infuriating. Lifting my hand, I smooth my thumb over the apple of her cheek, a bruise already forming. "And how did you get this?"

She looks at the space between us before whispering, "He hit me."

I bite down on my tongue, fury roaring in my chest. When I feel that I have control of my tone, I reply, "Then as far as I'm concerned, he got off easy."

Shaking her head, she rolls her eyes. "Assault doesn't justify murder, Massimo."

My hand snakes around the back of her neck, pulling her into me as my thumb traces over her jaw. "It does in my world, especially when the person being assaulted is *my wife*. I am your husband, Margot, and so long as you have my name and wear my rings, I will protect you how I see fit."

Her eyes search mine before she speaks, her voice nothing more than a breathless whisper when she says, "Understood."

Chapter 25

Margot

It's been a week since the incident at the club. Massimo and I have fallen into somewhat of a routine. He's gone by morning, and I hardly see him all day, but at night, he comes to me, using my body and burrowing his way into my bloodstream.

I would never admit it to him, but feeling his body on mine and the euphoric haze he leaves me with has staved off the nightmares.

Still, flashes of the man they called Russo, lying dead with eyes lifeless and blood pooling on his forehead, haunt me. I haven't told Massimo, not because I think he'll blame himself, but because I don't want him to think I'm weak. What happened that night was a normal occurrence for him. *It might very well become one for me too.* The thought sends a flare of panic up my spine until it's gripping my throat.

I jerk to the left, ignoring the shouts from the crowd on the busy New York sidewalk until I reach the edge of the curb. I bend at the waist, wrapping an arm around my middle as I claw at my neck with the other.

"You okay?" Daniele's feet appear in my line of sight, his large hand coming to rest on my shoulder.

Fuck.

Heat creeps up my neck, coloring my face as I straighten. Rubbing my hands down the front of my jeans, I meet his gaze before looking away. His concern is almost worse than if he had laughed.

"Absolutely fine," I reply, turning and marching toward the store we've come to a stop in front of. I'm on a mission to find a dress, and the quicker I do that, the sooner I can get home and curl up in the library with a book.

My vision is tunneled, focused on my destination rather than my surroundings, and I only make it five steps before I collide with a pedestrian. "I'm so sorry." I grimace when I realize just how crowded the sidewalk is. My eyes drop to the hand on my elbow, a hand with a familiar scar across the thumb. *The one I used to trace with my fingertip.* "Ethan?" I whisper, sure I'm imagining him, even as my gaze jumps around his face. He's still as handsome as I remember but my body doesn't react like it once did. Still, I find comfort in seeing him again after all this time. "I thought..." *That Massimo had killed you.* "How... What are you doing here?"

A sad smile ghosts his lips before his focus shifts over my shoulder. He releases me, stuffing his hands into his jacket pockets, a shutter coming down in his eyes. "Hey, M."

I step toward him, reaching out for the lapels of his worn leather jacket, but he takes a step back and my arms fall limply to my sides. "I've been trying to text you but my messages aren't..." I trail off, the desperation in my words obvious to my own ears.

Scrubbing a hand over the back of his neck, Ethan looks at the ground. His embarrassment matches my own. "Yeah." He drags out the word before continuing, "Your husband paid me a visit and blocked your number."

"Oh." *Of course Massimo would do that.* I was right about him and I'd do well to remember that. Seeing Ethan now reminds me of the life I'll never get back. I want to tell him that I'm sorry, that I still love him and probably always will, but the words won't come.

I turn away, my eyes stinging with unshed tears that I refuse to shed. Over my shoulder, I call, "Well, it was nice seeing you. Take care."

I reach the curb as a white van with blacked-out windows pulls up. The side door slides open, revealing a man wearing a balaclava and dressed in black. He steps out, his eyes locked on me. I stare at him, shock rooting my feet to the asphalt. Everything around me distorts, the once vibrant city now muted. My mind screams at me to run, but I can't move.

In one swift motion, I'm dragged behind Daniele, screams filling the air as three of Massimo's men appear with their weapons drawn. Daniele speaks into his phone, his words urgent as he demands for the car to be brought to our location. My pulse pounds in my ears, frantic and uneven as I try to process what's just happened.

Tires squeal and I peer around Daniele just in time to see the van swerving between cars as it speeds down the street before driving onto the sidewalk and out of view.

"Get on the floor," Daniele barks to the man from the van, authority in every word. "Keep your hands where I can see them." His arms are lifted and I imagine his gun trained on him.

I dart a glance around Daniele, finding Angelo kneeling beside one of the attackers, now face down on the ground. He secures the zip-ties around the man's wrists with practiced precision.

Within seconds, one of our blacked-out SUVs roars to the curb, ignoring the honking of the vehicles it cuts off. Another man jumps out, walking to the back of the car and opening the trunk. Three of Massimo's men carry the man on the ground, shoving him inside.

I look around at the bystanders staring. Some have their phones out and are recording, others are no doubt calling the police. *Holy shit.* This is my first real glimpse at the danger of Massimo's world. Someone nearly took me and if they'd have been successful, there wouldn't have been a damn thing I could do to escape. *Is Massimo safe, or was it just me they're targeting?*

In the chaos of my thoughts, my attention jumps to Ethan. His slack jaw tells of his shock and likely mirroring my own. *Will he be safe?* I should have paid more attention to my surroundings. Massimo has told me people are after him, and yet, I've relied on others to keep me safe. What if somebody with ill intentions had seen Ethan talking to me? I left to keep him safe and now I could have put him in harm's way without even thinking.

"Get in the front seat, Margot," Daniele commands. His voice is calm but I don't miss the undercurrent of steel. He doesn't look at me, his focus is on the surrounding buildings, surveilling them. A chill runs down my spine, the cold efficiency of how Daniele has handled this situation a reminder of who he is.

I rush to the car, climbing into the passenger seat and shutting the door behind me. Renato has the car moving before Angelo and Daniele have had time to fully close their doors. I'm slammed into my seat, the air knocked from my lungs as we travel at speed toward the outskirts of the city. The sound of horns blaring and people yelling follows in our wake.

The muffled yells from the man in the trunk blend with the hum of the engine, his panicked thuds a haunting soundtrack for the life I find myself trapped in. Being married to Massimo isn't the only threat I face. Today has shown me that his enemies are watching and waiting for the perfect moment to strike.

I squeeze my eyes shut, leaning my head against the cool window as the city passes us in a blur and I try to douse the wildfire of dread in my stomach. I don't know how much more of this I can take. But what's the alternative? *Death?*

Chapter 26

Massimo

S houting pulls my attention away from the emails
I'm reviewing. I know my men can handle whatever it is, but the commotion goes on for longer
than I expect, becoming louder as it moves from the
driveway to the house.

Unholstering my weapon, I move with caution across
the living room, pressing my back to the wall and peering
out of the window. A sinking sensation fills me, and I
abandon the idea of a sneak attack when I spot my SUV
in the driveway. *The same one that I sent Margot into the
city in.*

I cross the room, flinging the door open and stepping
into the entryway. My nostrils flare and I prepare to tear
into whichever bastard is responsible for whatever the
fuck has happened.

Daniele walks through the front door. "Boss." He
heads toward the door that leads to the basement.

185

"What the fuck has happened, and where is Margot?"

Daniele faces me and I catch the hesitation that he isn't quite quick enough to mask. "There was an attempted kidnapping—"

I huff out a breath, turning away from him and balling my fists. Relief battles with rage in my chest, a volatile mix that threatens to suffocate me. *How the fuck did this happen?* Daniele's word should be enough, but I find myself moving toward the stairs, certain she'll have found solace in the library.

"We have one of the men."

I halt and slowly turn to face him. "You could have led with that." Looking over my shoulder at the top of the steps, I ask, "Is she okay?" I should be indifferent when it comes to her, but there's an uncomfortable weight that settles on my chest at the notion that she'd come to harm. Margot has come to mean something to me, that much is clear, but I'm not sure I'm ready to unpack the extent of it.

"They never touched her. I think she's stronger than any of us have given her credit for."

Given the events of this past week, Margot's strength is not something I feel the need to question. Not bothering to respond to his statement, I pass him as I head for the basement. Daniele follows behind me, his support unwavering.

The door closes behind us, each step I take down the dimly lit corridor drawing on the darkness within me. It seeps into my body until it's consuming me and I don't feel fully in control of myself. He's going to tell me who sent them and then he will pay with his life.

The smell of urine and stale blood hangs in the air. It's a familiar scent in this part of the house, a constant reminder of those who have tried to cross generations of my family.

At the nearest open cell, I find a man tied to the metal chair that is bolted to the floor. His eyes are covered by what I assume was the balaclava he wore to conceal his identity. It's rolled up to reveal only the bridge of his nose and down creating a blindfold.

Daniele shuts and bolts the door before removing the mask. I watch the terror flare in the man's gaze, the corner of my mouth lifting in a twisted smirk. He glances at his bound hands, attempting to free himself. The panic makes his movements jerky.

"Who sent you?" I demand, pushing away from the wall to circle him.

He lifts his chin before his face twists into an ugly sneer. There goes the fear I thrive on and in comes the '*fuck it*' that makes this much less fun.

"Fuck you," he spits, a slight accent to his tone. The silence builds, his insult hanging in the air.

Nodding, I approach him, my steps slow and languid as I roll up the sleeves of my shirt. "I take it, you know who I am?"

"Yes," he snarls.

I move to the counter that runs along the wall opposite the door. An array of tools is laid out before me. I have my choice of torture device, but it's the rusty spoon that draws my attention.

Turning back to him, I hold it up, and he laughs, the sound hollow but lacking the bravado I'm certain he meant. Closing the distance between us in less than a second, I grab a fistful of his hair and yank his head back.

"You think this is funny?" I snarl, pressing my cheek to his and bringing the spoon closer to his face. "Do you have any idea of what I am capable of?" I pause; the silence sitting heavy between us. "Well, you can multiply whatever you're thinking by ten because you targeted *her*."

He swallows, the fear returning to his eyes. Shoving his head away, I straighten, reining in the monster inside of me who's begging to be freed. *Not yet.*

I toy with the spoon, picking up a blow torch and heating the rusted metal. My eyes are fixed on him, his fear feeding the monster inside of me. I need to find out who sent him, if I kill him without that information, Margot will never be safe. "I will ask you again. Who sent you?"

He doesn't say a word, his eyes on the wall ahead of him.

Throwing the spoon onto the counter, I draw back my fist before slamming it into his cheek. Pain radiates through my knuckles, but it's worth it to watch his head snap back and his eyes go glassy.

I lean down until my face is inches from his. "You

came for my wife. Now tell me who sent you, or this will be your last conversation," I bite, my frustration mounting by the second.

"Kill me if you want, but it won't stop more from coming," he spits.

Daniele steps forward, grabbing the guy's hair and forcing his head down. He yanks the collar of his sweater, revealing a tattoo. One I know all too well.

Fedeltà Eterna: Eternal Loyalty.

Elio Moretti. Which means, that despite having gone underground, he's still making a play for my family. The tattoo is the brand his men receive when they join his ranks. It's a reminder that every move they make is done with *him* at the forefront. He's still making moves on us, and I have no doubt he planned to use Margot to get his way, just like he tried and failed with Aurora.

A sense of calm washes over me at the confirmation. I no longer have a use for this fucker. Returning to the counter, I retrieve the rusty spoon, rolling it between my fingers. "You might not want to tell me anything, but your ink has given me everything I need. I know who sent you and why."

He twists in the chair, trying to look at us. With a subtle nod from me, Daniele steps forward, clamping his arm around the guy's neck and holding him in a choke-hold. I step in, brandishing the spoon. At the sight, he thrashes in Daniele's hold, but with his limbs bound, there's no escape.

Standing beside him, I bring the spoon to his eye,

digging it into the inner corner. He cries out, bucking in the chair, but I just press deeper. A squelching pop reverberates around the room and his body goes limp as the spoon slides behind the back of his eyeball, fracturing the orbital bone.

His eye swings lazily at his cheekbone and his ragged breaths rattle in his throat. The sight of him does little to quell my anger. Watching him squirm might have felt like I was reclaiming a sliver of control, but in reality, he was just a pawn. *It wasn't enough.* Nothing will be enough until Elio Moretti pays in blood.

Dropping the spoon onto the counter, I lock eyes with Daniele as he releases the man. "Finish him, get rid of his body and then meet me in my office. We need to strategize."

"Yes, boss."

I head back into the house, fury still coursing through my veins.

This is the first proper attack—or at least attempt at one—since we rescued Aurora from the warehouse. Do they think they'll do more damage, or get what they want by going after Margot? It's clear she's their target now, and if that is the case, then Elio Moretti will pay.

I won't rest until I've taken him, and every single one of his men out because she's mine and nobody touches what's mine.

Chapter 27

Massimo

I find Margot in the library, as expected. It's been hours since she returned, since I ended a man's life. I thought I would give her space to process what's happened today, but in truth, I've needed the time to calm the anger simmering under my skin. It's still there, the embers of my fury refusing to die down.

He thought he could take her from me. That he could put his fucking hands on what's mine and walk away. Elio Moretti tried to send a message today, and I replied in blood.

Standing on the threshold, I watch Margot in the reflection of the window for a moment; her features relaxed and portraying none of the disquiet I thought I would find. She's staring out, watching the branches of the trees dance in the light breeze. With every second that passes, I feel the ugly clawing of my fury. *She's still here, still mine, but for how long?*

I stride into the room, enveloping myself in her scent as it blends with the old books in my grandfather's library. As I approach the couch, she moves to make space for me. We don't speak, instead, I lift her feet into my lap and massage the soles.

The tension seeps out of my body, and I rest my head on the back of the couch, looking at her through my lashes. I see the shadows under her eyes and her exhaustion in the slight curve of her shoulders.

Squeezing her foot, I wait for her to look at me before saying, "I am sorry that you had to go through what you did today."

Her tongue darts out to wet her lips and she nods slowly. "You killed him."

It's not a question but a statement.

"Yes."

She scoffs, looking back to the window. "You didn't even hesitate."

Cracking my neck, I let the silence hang in the air, heavy and thick. She's looking for something in me that just isn't there. *Something that I can't give her*. Regret, shame, an apology. I'm not sure exactly what, but I can't be that man. Won't be that man.

"I won't lie to you, Margot. He was a threat to us. To you." I pause, and she meets my gaze, "and because of that, I had to act."

She shakes her head. "But at what cost?"

My jaw tightens, but I force my body to remain relaxed. "It doesn't matter. My only concern is the safety of my family and doing whatever it takes to protect that. You are safe."

She laughs, but it lacks humor. "Until the next time. Because let's be honest, someone will try again."

To an extent, she's right, but certainty coats my words when I reply. "I'll do everything in my power to ensure your safety, Margot."

She stands, pulling her cardigan tighter around her body. "I appreciate that, Massimo." Something flickers in her gaze, but I can't grasp what it is before it's gone. "Today has been a lot to process and I'm tired, so I'm going to bed," she says softly, avoiding eye contact.

I scrub a hand over my jaw, exhaling heavily as I sit forward. "I just wanted to make sure you were okay."

A small smile lifts the corners of her mouth, and she meets my gaze. "I'm fine. It was unexpected, but I know that Daniele and the others had me covered."

I search her gaze for any hint that she might not be telling the truth about being okay, but come up empty. She walks past me, my fingers brushing against hers as she goes. It's a silent gesture, but also my reassurance that she's still here. They didn't get her and I'm doing everything I can as her husband to keep her safe.

I'd kill a million men if it meant I'd get to keep her.

Chapter 28

Margot

Massimo's words circle in my head like a record as I walk the quiet corridors to our bedroom. My skin still tingles from his touch, his presence lingering even though he's no longer here.

You are safe.

His words should be a comfort, but they only unsettle me because I know they're not true. This isn't the first attempt they have made at taking me and I'm certain it won't be the last. It's that fact that fills me with uncertainty and fear. I'll never truly be safe for as long as I am married to Massimo. Someone will always be looking to ruin him.

But would they achieve that by taking me?

I honestly don't know.

Slipping into the bedroom, I cross the room, the

silence suffocating. I go through the motions of undressing and pulling my T-shirt over my naked body. Ignoring my racing thoughts, I brush my teeth before crawling under the covers and flicking off the bedside lamp. I stare at the ceiling, sinking into my exhaustion, even though I know sleep won't come easily for me tonight.

My mind drifts back to what Ethan had said before everything went down. *Would Massimo really have threatened him?* Who am I kidding? Ethan never lied to me and Massimo just killed a man for trying to kidnap me.

So why didn't I confront Massimo about what he did to Ethan?

That should have been the first thing I did when we returned, or at least when Massimo found me in the library. Instead, all I could think about was how safe I felt in his presence; how his hands on my skin grounded me when they should have repulsed me. And it's not just tonight. The truth is, Massimo should terrify me, given everything I know about him. But when he's near, I feel anything but afraid. Instead, there is just anticipation and a rush of excitement.

I exhale sharply, turning onto my side and punching my pillow to fluff it. What the hell is wrong with me? I don't want to be a woman who bends to the will of her husband. Or become someone who's blinded to the danger he exudes because she's intoxicated by how he makes her feel. But I don't want to leave. I feel a pull toward him. And it's that conflict burning inside of me that unravels me in ways I never expected.

If I don't put a stop to it, will I even recognize myself anymore?

Tomorrow, when I've had time to process the attempted kidnapping and I'm firing on all cylinders mentally, I'll confront Massimo about Ethan and make him see that he can't control me or my life.

Chapter 29

Massimo

The dessert plates have been cleared; the restaurant near to closing time. It's been a pleasant evening if I ignore Margot glaring at me for a good portion of it. Of course, she's sweet as honey to Antonio Rizzo and his wife, Gia, but whenever they're wrapped up in conversation with each other, Margot's expression morphs into pure disgust, aimed solely at me.

I suspect it has something to do with her near kidnapping that we have yet to talk about, at least properly. But it could also be because I've dared to breathe the same air as her. I can never tell what to expect from my wife.

"Do you two have honeymoon plans?" Gia asks, her features softened by the bottle of wine she's drank.

Margot lifts her glass to her lips, muttering something that sounds a lot like, "Not a chance."

I reach for her hand, gripping it hard enough to get

197

my message across: *Behave.* It's the one request I made on the twenty-minute drive here. Antonio and Gia live near me, so it made sense for us to meet somewhere local rather than trek into New York City.

With my free hand, I swirl the wine in my glass, leaning back in my seat. "I'm sure we will go on one eventually, but now isn't the time."

Antonio nods, sympathy and understanding filling his features. "You've had a lot to deal with, that's for sure. I have no doubt that you have everything in hand, but I would still like the opportunity to discuss an allegiance. Perhaps we can get together next week to talk?"

Attacks or not, Antonio has been pushing for a family alliance since I took over from my father. For all I know, he could be part of the plot against us. Much like in a game of poker, I need to keep my cards close to my chest. I can't trust anyone in this world, least of all a man who tells me he wants to help.

"Let's not discuss business tonight," I say, glancing around the restaurant before meeting his gaze again. "Besides, I'm certain things will be reaching a resolution by the end of the week." A lie, but I keep my face neutral.

"That's good to hear," he replies, his fingers tapping on the tabletop before Gia covers them with her palm.

A hush falls over the table when he leans into her, speaking in low tones. I seize the opportunity to wrap my hand around the back of Margot's neck, my grip firm and uncompromising. Pulling her into me, I press my forehead against hers, the action deceptively intimate for anyone who cares to watch.

"Whatever is going on with your attitude tonight, get rid of it. I won't think twice about bending you over my knee and smacking it out of you, Margot. I don't give a shit if it's in the middle of this fucking restaurant." My tone brokers no argument, but I know she'll try.

She pulls back as much as my hold will let her, resting her hand on my chest over my heart. I force my body to relax, conveying none of the frustration that has been simmering inside me as the evening has gone on.

Margot tilts her head, her lips pulling into a smile that doesn't reach her eyes. "I'd like to see you try," she purrs, walking her fingers up my chest. She hooks one into the collar where I've left the top two buttons undone, skimming them over my bare skin. "There isn't a chance that you'd mess up this dinner." She loops her arms around my neck, stroking her fingers through the hair at my nape. Her lips ghost over the shell of my ear as she continues, "If you had wanted a compliant wife, then you picked the wrong person. I don't take kindly to the people I care about being threatened and cut out of my life behind my back."

I fall back into my seat, forcing her to release me and pick up my glass of wine, draining the contents before setting it on the table. Tossing my napkin next to it, I stand, pulling a wad of cash from my pocket and throwing a couple of hundred dollars onto the tabletop. I feel Antonio and Gia staring at me and when I slide the remaining cash back into my pocket, I lift my head giving them a polite nod.

"It's been a wonderful evening but there is something I need to take care of."

Without waiting for a reply, I grab Margot's arm, forcing her to stand and haul her from the restaurant. If she wants to behave like a petulant child, I'll punish her like one. The thought sends a thrill racing through me. It's always explosive whenever we come together with our anger at the forefront. And I, for one, can't fucking wait.

Outside, my Bugatti sits at the curb. "We'll meet you at the house," I instruct my men, who jump into action at our abrupt exit.

A hint of what looks like surprise passes through his gaze, but without question, Daniele, who was waiting in the bar, heads for the SUV parked behind my car. I've never deviated from a plan, let alone told my men to leave me. But there's something I need to do and it doesn't require an audience.

Opening the passenger door, I wait for Margot to climb in. She huffs out a breath but doesn't say a word. Urgency claws at my skin, demanding that I reclaim some of the control that seems to have slipped from my grasp. Every time she pushes back, I feel like I lose a little more.

Sliding into the driver's seat, I fire up the engine, the roar it releases is powerful and calls to my frustration.

Without checking that she's buckled in, I peel away

from the curb, my tires squealing. It doesn't take long for us to reach the winding roads that lead home. My foot grows heavier on the pedal, the car taking the corners with ease.

Margot's delicate fingers hold on to my forearm, squeezing for my attention as she pleads, "Massimo, slow down."

I only ease up on the gas when the turn I need appears ahead. We leave behind the main highway and travel along a gravel single-track lane. This car wasn't made for a road like this. We creep along at an agonizingly slow pace, the quiet punctured by the sound of stones clinking under the chassis.

About a third of the way up the track, I pull over, killing the engine and plunging us into darkness. The moon overhead casts a pale light across the night sky, and when I look at Margot, her eyes are wide with what looks like trepidation. It radiates off her in waves.

Good.

"Get out of the car." My voice is low and controlled, nothing like how I feel inside.

She shakes her head. "No."

I close my eyes, blowing out a breath before growling, "Get out of the *fucking* car, Margot."

Her movements are hurried as she fumbles with the door handle. Once she's out, I exit, shrugging out of my jacket and laying it on my seat.

"This way," I instruct, nodding toward the tree line.

Margot looks at me, then over to the forest before

returning her eyes to me. I can practically hear her mind working overtime, considering whether or not she should make a run for it.

In the dim light, I see her throat work, my cock twitching at the idea of wrapping my hand around it. She blows out a breath, wrapping her arms around her waist before she lifts her chin and walks in the direction I've indicated.

Her hatred for me in this moment burns bright, threatening to turn me to ash. And yet, I'll gladly walk into her fire.

"If you're going to kill me, make it quick," she snaps.

I don't respond. Let her think that's what I'm going to do, maybe she'll be a little more compliant. The corner of my mouth lifts at the idea of her doing as I demand without question.

When we reach the trees, Margot hesitates, looking over her shoulder at me. She must see an answer on my face to the question that's swimming in her gaze, because she steps forward, disappearing into the shadows. I follow, some of the tension from earlier seeping out of me. Almost immediately, my nostrils fill with the scent of damp earth and pine.

My nonno used to bring me to this forest for target practice. I know these woods like the back of hand, the clearing up ahead perfect for what I have planned.

Margot comes to a stop in the middle of the space, dropping her arms to her sides.

With my hands in my pockets, I circle her, cataloging

every curve, every minute detail, trying to commit it to memory. *Fuck. She's really something.* "You said something back at the restaurant."

She closes her eyes, dipping her chin before lifting it and looking at me. "Yes."

"Remind me what it was," I say, my tone calm and almost cajoling.

"Do we really have to do this?"

I come to a stop in front of her. "Humor me."

Her eyes drop to the gun holstered to my chest, and I catch the flare of anxiety. I grip her chin, forcing her to keep her eyes on my face.

"I said you picked the wrong wife if you were looking for someone compliant to your needs," she breathes.

I bare my teeth in a false grin. "That's not quite what I was looking for. You told me that you didn't take kindly to people being threatened and forced out of your life."

She remains silent, her eyes fluttering as she tries to hide from me. "Look at me, Margot," I demand, an edge to my tone. Reluctantly, she stares at me, the embers of a fire sparking in the depths. "I didn't make any threats. I made promises." My grip tightens a fraction before I release her and step back. "Tell me, what do you see around you?"

Rubbing her hands over her thighs, she looks around. "Nothing."

"Exactly." I move behind her, pressing my body to hers and snaking my hand around her waist, coming to a stop just under her breast.

Caging her in, uncaring that she can feel the hardness of my cock pressed into the softness of her ass, I murmur into her hair, "If I wanted to kill you, I could, and nobody would hear your screams or the thud of your body as it fell to the floor." She sucks in a shaky breath, her body tensing before she forces herself to relax. "You are *my wife*, and so long as you remember that, Margot, I will not harm you. But I will do whatever needs to be done to protect *our marriage*."

"I'm sorry." Her words are so faint, I can't be sure I didn't imagine them. An illusion would make more sense than Margot apologizing.

"Stop fighting me at every turn." I don't bother to hide my exasperation. After all, it's just the two of us here.

Her head tips back when I lift my hand to cup her breast. *At least in this way we work.* I knead the mound, leaning in to dust my lips over the space behind her ear. Margot moans, her hips grinding against me. It's the little mewls falling from her lips that send me over the edge.

I yank up the hem of her dress, my movements rushed and desperate. My teeth graze her shoulder as my fingers seek out her clit, cursing under my breath when I find her naked beneath her dress.

"Massimo," Margot cries out when I flick the swollen bud. She reaches back, hooking an arm around my neck and arching her spine.

"You're so fucking wet," I groan when her ass presses into my painfully hard cock.

I slide two fingers through her folds, sinking them into her with ease. Margot turns her face toward me, gasping breaths escaping her parted lips. I can't resist closing the gap and swiping my tongue into her mouth.

We devour each other with hungry kisses, like this might be the last time. She tastes like the chocolate cake she had at dinner, but more importantly, she tastes like she belongs to *me*.

When we part, our breaths are labored, and the only sound I can hear in the quiet of the woods. *I need to be inside her. Now.* Guiding Margot to the nearest tree, my voice is raw when I grunt, "Hold on."

She bends at the waist, giving me the perfect view of her bare pussy. Her arousal is clear, glistening under the moonlight.

Desperation fuels me, and I yank my zipper down, before stepping behind her and running my cock through her slick heat. Margot moans as I groan, the friction electrifying.

Fuck, she feels good.

I ease in slowly, her warmth enveloping me. The base of my spine tingles, the sensation a warning of how dangerously close to the edge I am. I dig my fingers into her hips, tipping my head back as I cry out, "Fuck."

Pulling back, I slam into her, the power of my thrust knocking her arms out from under her. Banding an arm around her waist, I pull her back as I pound into her until black dots dance in my vision.

"Massimo."

God. My name on her lips sends me hurtling faster toward the edge of my release. It just might be the best fucking thing I've ever heard. Margot reaches back, her fingers grazing my thighs and urging me on.

"So fucking good," I growl, my body tightening in anticipation.

I don't think I could stop even if I tried.

Pained groans spill from me. Within seconds, her walls clamp down, milking my cock. My balls draw up, and I cum with a strangled cry, burying myself in her as deep as I can and emptying inside of her.

She's going to be the fucking death of me. And the worst part? I don't think I'd want to stop it.

Chapter 30

A light breeze skims over the backs of my bare thighs, shoving me back into reality. *Did that really just happen?* I honestly thought Massimo had brought me here to put a bullet in me, but instead, he *claimed* me, and I liked it.

How can he make me so angry, or scared and then aroused? Life with him is like a roller coaster, there are so many ups and downs, but I keep coming back for more. I keep seeking out that thrill.

The scent of pine and raw earth mixes with the musky tang of sex, the damp spring air a stark contrast to the heat of what we just did. Our combined release spills from me, dripping onto the forest floor when Massimo pulls out, leaving me empty. I still feel him on my skin, like a phantom imprint of his touch, and yet, I crave more.

The noise of his zipper gliding up breaks the stillness,

somehow reverberating through the trees. Standing, I fix my dress, biting my lower lip at the delicious ache between my legs. I've never felt this way before. Even though he can piss me off, I have a fierce desire for my husband, to feel him on me, and inside of me.

It's so different to how it was with Ethan.

I swallow, waiting for the guilt to drown me, but it doesn't come, and the memories of him are starting to feel distant, like what we shared was a lifetime ago.

Massimo reaches for me, straightening the neckline of my dress and drawing my focus back to him. His knuckles graze my collarbone, sending a tremor of need through my body. I've just had him, and yet I want him again.

My eyes search his, looking for... something. Maybe a sign that he's as confused as I am by what's going on between us.

Reaching out, I rest my hand on his chest. "I should have talked to you about how I was feeling."

He brushes a stray lock of my hair back, tucking it behind my ear. "You should have."

Of course that's his response. Why wouldn't it be? God forbid he actually admitted that what he did was wrong. Rolling my eyes, I step back, but he wraps an arm around my waist and holds me close.

"You shouldn't have interfered in my life." I huff.

He tips his head back, scanning the thick canopy of trees overhead before returning his focus to me.

It's dark, and I can't read his expression, but I press

on. "For as long as we're married, I will be faithful, Massimo. But I have known Ethan for most of my life. You can't expect me to—"

He raises a brow and lifts my left hand, letting his thumb glide over the backs of my wedding bands. The possessiveness of the action quickens my pulse, and I lower my lashes to hide my excitement from him.

"It appears that I need to clarify a few things. *One*: 'Til death do us part is exactly how this marriage will end. *Two*: I can, and I will, expect you to cut off anyone who has romantic feelings for you. *That* is non-negotiable. *Three*: If Ethan truly wanted you, he wouldn't have sat there silently, watching as you vowed yourself to *me*."

He's impossible. "You're impossible," I huff. "This isn't the 1800s; you can't dictate my life for me."

Massimo's hold on me tightens, then eases slightly. "You might not see it now, but everything I do is to protect you, Margot. As your husband, that is my job but you make it increasingly difficult when you fight with me over every decision I make."

I shove at his chest, but he doesn't budge, fueling my irritation. "Because you make decisions *for me* rather than *with me*," I snap, before forcing myself to control my tone. "That's all I want. For my husband to include me in the decision-making process about things that could impact me, or our marriage. Like an equal, like he views me as his partner instead of his subordinate."

Massimo exhales heavily, as if my request is an

annoyance and something he would never consider doing. Then he lets me go. The weight of disappointment slams into me and I step around him, shaking my head. *I want to go home.*

I barely take three steps back toward the car before he catches my hand, threading his fingers with mine and halting me. With my back to him, I wait for him to say something, my eyes trained on the shadows ahead even as my heart thuds a chaotic beat.

His voice is low, a note of reluctance in his tone when he says, "Where I can, I will discuss things with you first. But that's not always going to be possible so you can't lose your shit or act out every time *you think* I should have told you something."

I guess that's better than nothing.

The start of our marriage has been mentally draining and I'm tired of constantly having to be on my guard. Inhaling, I turn to face him, forcing him to release my hand. It's not exactly what I want, especially as he can use it as an excuse whenever it suits him, but what choice do I have? It's either this or we carry on as we have been, butting heads until one of us 'wins'.

Stepping forward, I hold my hand out between us, biting down on my bottom lip when Massimo slides his warm and slightly calloused palm into mine. "Deal. No more fighting." I flutter my lashes before lightly adding, "For now, anyway."

He scoffs, giving my arm a playful yank that brings

me flush against his chest. My free hand rests between us over the steady beat of his heart.

Massimo dips his head, and my eyes shut of their own accord. "With my wife," he murmurs, his voice thick with desire and stirring a heat in my core, "I seal deals with a kiss, not a handshake."

His mouth claims mine in a searing kiss. It steals the breath from my lungs and my knees buckle beneath me. But Massimo is there to catch me, tightening his hold and devouring my mouth with a hunger that matches my own.

Gasping, I lean back, gazing into his darkened gaze. "If we aren't fighting anymore, does that mean we have to have boring sex in a bed?"

He slides his hand down my back and over my ass, grabbing at the flesh. His mouth stretches into a wide, wolfish grin against my mouth. "Not a fucking chance."

Thank fuck.

Chapter 31

Margot

I stretch, arching my back as I push my arms above my head. I've just had the coziest nap, lulled to sleep by the patter of rain outside. Between the fireplace's warmth and my own fatigue, I was powerless.

Tucking my hands under my cheek, I roll onto my side, watching the fat droplets sliding down the window from the stormy gray sky above. *It feels like all it's done is rain since I moved in here.*

When it's quiet like this, and all I can hear is the rain hitting the glass and the wood crackling in the fireplace, it's not hard to pretend my life is something it isn't. That the sins of those around me don't exist and that everything is sunshine and roses.

Exhaling, I push up onto my elbow, peeking over the couch's arm at the clock on the bookshelf behind the desk. *Three hours* have gone. One minute I was reading, half listening for the rat to make an appearance, and the next minute, I dozed off. Standing, I gather my books, moving to the shelves to slide them back into place. If I have missed them, then I'll come back tomorrow and the day after that. I won't stop until I figure out who I've been overhearing.

They'll come back around, it's just going to be a matter of time and I can't *live* in this room while I wait for that to happen. Besides, Alma's serving dinner at six, and I promised Massimo I'd be on time, unlike the last couple of evenings.

After tossing some trash in the can, I grab my water bottle on the way to the door, ready to head back to my room and get washed up for dinner. I swing open the door and step into the corridor, colliding with a wall of muscle.

I stumble back into the library, my arms coming up to claw at the wall in an attempt to steady myself. It doesn't go unnoticed that whoever I've knocked into, doesn't care if I land on my ass.

When I find my balance, I huff out a breath, my gaze travels from the pinstripe pants to the matching blazer and crisp white shirt open at the collar. Cold, hard eyes sweep over me before his thin lips flatten in disgust. I stiffen, the hairs on the back of my neck standing on end.

Aldo.

This guy gives me the creeps. He has from the first day I met him. I take a step forward, expecting him to move but he doesn't. His large frame blocks the doorway and I gulp down the sour taste of dread in my mouth. As I stare at him, he puts a small black flip phone into his pocket.

"How long have you been in there?" He inclines his head to the room behind me. His voice is clipped and controlled like he's trying to hide something.

I glance back at the library and the daylight that's fought its way through the clouds and into the room. It's a stark contrast to the man in front of me. Returning my focus to him, I tilt my head, my brows tugging together, when I reply, "I don't know. A few hours?" *Why does he care?*

He darts his attention to the end of the corridor then back to me before stepping closer. Something dark and sinister flickers across his features, a flash of what I can only describe as pure evil. If this was a scary movie, I'd be hiding behind my cushion.

"Stay out of the library, Margot." There's a hint of panic in his voice, but it vanishes when he adds, "I'd hate for something to happen because you heard something you shouldn't."

Hell no. Who does he think he is, trying to intimidate me in *my own home*? A spark of defiance surges through me and I fold my arms, moving closer until we're inches apart.

"That's funny," I say, tapping my chin. "Massimo didn't say anything about staying out of here, which is strange, right? Considering he's been in here with me every night this week."

Aldo steps back, his jaw working as he grinds his teeth. "When was he in there?" he demands.

Rolling my eyes, I push past him, striding down the corridor and calling over my shoulder, "Why don't you ask him? Or is it none of your damn business?" My pulse thrums in my ears.

This is Massimo's world, filled with his men and enemies, both as dangerous as each other. *I should be more careful*. He might have promised to protect me, and I know he will—we've grown closer since the night in the woods— but what happens if they take him out? My chest constricts at the thought, and an emotion I can't name rushes through me. Someone in his home is plotting against him, but will Massimo be victorious? I honestly don't know.

On my way to my room, I replay the interaction with Aldo. *The whole exchange was off.* Why was he so on edge? Is *he* the man that I overheard outside of the library the other day? No. That would be the ultimate betrayal to Massimo. *And make Aldo a dangerous enemy to have.* Did I make a mistake by being dismissive?

Now that Massimo and I have reached some semblance of peace, maybe I should tell him what I've overheard. I might not have many specifics, but what I do have could be the missing puzzle piece in their investigation and help them find whoever is trying to take him out.

But what if he doesn't believe me?

I gnaw on my bottom lip, torn between telling him and waiting. If I hold off and something happens, I don't know how I'd live with that. But if I do tell him and he dismisses me, then I find more later, will he listen to me? Sighing, I force the worry aside and focus on dinner.

One more day, I decide. If I don't find anything else out, I'll tell him what I know.

That's all I can do.

Chapter 32

Massimo

I stare at my left hand, idly spinning my wedding band with my thumb. Ever since the night Margot was assaulted in my club, I've kept it on. Something about it affirms my commitment to her, to us. I'm far more accustomed to the feel of it on my finger than I thought I would be.

"Massimo?" Daniele calls, his voice snapping me back to reality.

Blinking, the room around me refocuses and I smooth my hand down my face before clearing my throat and readjusting my position in my chair. "Yes?"

Daniele leans over, muting the landline on my desk. "Luigi wants to know if we're accepting the offer from the Russians?"

I nod and unmute the phone. "We have no reason to accept Kuznetsov's offer. It's an insult more than anything. In fact, I'm certain that they've lowballed us

217

to see how desperate we are and I have no intention of negotiating with them after this stunt. I suggest you stay clear, Luigi, or risk losing everything your family built."

Luigi sighs, sounding like a man at his breaking point. He's been the head of his family since before I was born. It's only natural that he would consider taking an offer that would grant him relief of what can sometimes feel like a burden. But I've always been taught to be wary of wolves in sheep's clothing, and that's exactly how the Russians operate. They want to take over our weapons importation, keep us partially involved, and push their own drug and human trafficking. Shit that I wouldn't touch with a ten-foot pole.

"I don't know, Massimo. Not all of us are as young as you. Besides, I have no family to leave this to. It wouldn't matter if they robbed me blind."

We fall quiet, the memory of Luigi's loss coating us in a blanket of darkness. His wife and three children were on a plane when it exploded midair. He lost everything that day, and what's worse is, the authorities have been unable to pinpoint the people responsible.

"It's your decision to make, Luigi. But DeMarco lost his entire area to them. Now they bring in their own guns and drugs, having cut him out entirely."

My attention shifts to Daniele with a question in my eyes. He lifts a shoulder, shaking his head, as puzzled as I am at why Luigi is even contemplating the offer.

"I'll take your advice into consideration, Massimo."

He pauses, and when I open my mouth, he continues, "I've been asked to speak to you about your wife."

My gaze flicks to the phone, as Daniele stands and crosses the room, shutting the door behind him as he leaves.

Once I'm sure we're alone, I ask, "What about my wife?" My annoyance is barely contained as I bite out the words.

There's a beat of hesitation before Luigi says, "Antonio informed us of your dinner." *God, they're like old ladies gossiping.* The heads of the other families in the tri-state area are Luigi, who they count on to deliver any bad news, Antonio, who surveys the situation and reports into Luigi, and Marco. He's the quieter one of the three, always watching and guarded.

"I'll come right out and say it, Massimo, she's a distraction to you, and because of that, she's a liability. Antonio said he's never seen you behave like you did the other night. You are the head of your family and she is young and inexperienced in our world. We promised your father when he passed that we would look out for you. God rest his soul."

I grind my jaw, biting my tongue to keep from snapping at him. *How fucking dare he?* If it were anyone else, I'd tell them exactly where they could shove their advice. But Luigi has my respect. *Barely.*

Forcing calm into my tone, I reply, "I'll take your advice into consideration." I know it won't be lost on Luigi that my response mirrors his own.

Silence greets me.

"Was there anything else?"

"No, nothing. Take care." Luigi sighs, cutting the call.

I blow out a breath and refocus on the contract I was studying. I will admit, Margot is a distraction. Hell, she's been on my mind and occupying my thoughts since the moment I knew of her existence, but she is my wife and Luigi had no right to discuss her with me. If she is a liability, she's mine.

My problem.

My responsibility.

My wife.

There's a knock on the door. "Come in," I call, my voice stiff.

Aldo enters, inclining his head as he crosses the room. "Boss."

I don't speak, instead, I pick up my pen and sign the contract in front of me and wait for him to say whatever it is he came in here to say. And it had better not be about Margot.

"I found Margot in the library and I know you gave strict instructions for nobody to be in there."

Squeezing my eyes shut, I drag my thumb and forefinger over them before pinching the bridge of my nose. "This house is as much hers as it is mine. She is free to go into any room she pleases, including yours."

Aldo smooths his hand over his tie before clearing his throat. "Of course, my apologies. It just caught me off guard that she was in there."

Why the hell would that 'catch him off guard'? I frown, but before I can question him, Daniele enters, his phone pressed to his ear.

Pulling it away, he taps the screen and sets it down on the polished surface of my desk. "Leonardo, we're all here."

"Okay," Leonardo replies, his voice sounding distant. "I've found Haven. She's…" he trails off. When he speaks again, his tone is dejected. "She's in the hospital."

In all the years we've worked together, I've never heard Leonardo sound like this. I sit forward, my focus on the screen, willing him to continue. All we're met with is background noise, and tension coils in my gut with every second that passes. "What's happened, Leonardo?" I urge.

"Christ," he mutters, before exhaling sharply. "She had an accident. The baby is fine, but she's unconscious and they might need to induce her." He pauses, the sounds of the hospital filling the line before he continues, "Look, boss, I know you need me back, but that's my baby. I can't…"

I cut him off. "Send the hospital details and I'll update her mom. She'll want to travel up, so just be prepared for her." Maria is still angry with me for sending her daughter away and I don't blame her. "Do whatever you need to do to bring Haven and the baby home safely, Leonardo."

"Thanks, Massimo." Someone calls his name. "The doctor's here, I've got to go, but I'll keep you updated."

The line disconnects and Daniele pockets his phone. "I didn't see that coming. Leonardo, a father. Who'd have thought?" He smirks.

My mouth twitches into some semblance of a smile, and I shake my head as I roll up the sleeves of my shirt. Turning the conversation back to business, I ask, "Any update on Anastasia? Preferably one where she isn't having your child."

Daniele barks out a laugh, the sound bouncing around the room. "Not a chance of that happening. It won't be my dick I'll be putting in her but my bullet."

My smile fades, images of Aurora when we found her curled up in the corner of the room, barely hanging on but ready to fight, flash through my mind. It's a fresh reminder of the torture she endured at the hands of Anastasia. My jaw tightens to the point of pain.

Anastasia's still out there.

Still breathing. But not for much longer.

Chapter 33

Margot

The weather is gloomy and it's been raining since I woke up this morning, so I've been exploring the house for the last couple of hours, but I'm bored. After all, there are only so many rooms that I can go into.

Maybe I can bug Alma into teaching me how to make her homemade cookies. I've been inhaling them like air, eating my anxiety over still not telling Massimo what I know. I know that I *need* to, but I just can't find the right time. With my mind made up, I head in the direction of the main staircase.

A hushed, urgent voice echoes through the space as I near the corner that leads to the main corridor. Pressing my back to the wall, I listen intently. In the reflection of a picture hanging on the wall across from me, I can see a man, half-hidden in an alcove. *He must not realize that the acoustics carry.*

"I'm certain they don't know, Elio." There's a pause as I assume Elio speaks. "No, his wife will not be an issue. I'm taking the necessary steps to keep her out of my way. Trust me, I have everything in hand. I've been assigned the investigation now and it'll be simple enough to put all of this on Mattia, so we can move forward with *our* plan." He pauses again. "I'll tell him that it must have been left by one of the men who died during the attack on your property."

It doesn't take a genius to figure out that he's talking about the envelope I found. The puzzle pieces fit, though I still feel like I'm missing a key piece. There is no doubt that whoever this is, is the rat that Massimo told me about.

The fact that he's leading the investigation means that it can only be one of two men—Daniele or Aldo. Those are the only two people in this house that have knowledge of the investigation, although I know which one I'd put my money on it being. But, the truth is, I can't be certain.

God, I wish I'd had more interactions with both of them.

I wish I could say that I recognize the voice alone. But I need to see his face with my own eyes. I have to confirm that it is definitely him before I accuse one of Massimo's closest confidants of plotting to take him down.

What I don't understand is *why?* Why plot to kill a man that you have worked with for however long, just so you can fall into line with another? It doesn't make sense.

Shaking my head, I focus back on the low-toned conversation, my eyes fixed on the reflection. *Come on, show me your face.* He shuffles slightly, and every inch of my body goes on high alert. I hold my breath, worried I'll give myself away, and slide down the wall a little more.

"No, nobody will know. If they do, you know that I will take care of them, just like I did Francesco. You have my word and my loyalty. *Fedeltà Eterna.*"

I make a mental note of the names—Elio, Mattia, and Francesco. Did whoever is behind this *kill* the guy called Francesco? Am I going to be next if they see me? I swallow down the bile and fear that rises in my throat.

The question is, what do I do with this information? I know that what I'm hearing is vital in unmasking the rat, but how does it fit into the bigger picture?

At the start of our marriage, I might have leveraged this information for my freedom, but now? I think of Massimo's hand on my throat, not as a threat, but as a vow. I think of the way he kissed me in the woods, the way he touches me like he owns me. And I think maybe... he does, and not just in the physical sense.

He has my heart.

The realization fills me with a cocktail of elation and melancholy.

Biting my lower lip, I force myself to focus on the conversation taking place a few feet from me and what I'm going to do about it. How do I tell Massimo that someone close to him is trying to cover up their obvious involvement in a plot to tear him down? I've had days to figure out the answer, but I'm still no closer.

"Elio, calm down. Rome wasn't built in a day and you can't expect to take down a man as connected as Massimo in one, either," he reassures, a confidence in his duplicity. "I have to go. Just trust that I have the situation in hand."

I keep my gaze locked on his reflection when his arm drops to his side. He steps from the alcove, glancing up and down the corridor. My eyes widen as he strides away with the confidence of man in his position. I knew it was him, but seeing it firsthand is almost paralyzing.

Nausea churns in my gut, my vision tunneling as the full weight of the truth crushes me. This is Massimo's right hand man. The person he trusts the most.

Aldo.

It's only when I can no longer hear his footsteps or see his retreating back in the glass that I suck in a breath, bending at the waist as panic washes over me like a rising tide.

Holy shit.

My body wants to run and scream but I can't move. Instead, I'm rooted to the spot, the responsibility of my discovery hanging over me like a black cloud.

Chapter 34

Massimo

When I enter our bedroom, Margot is pacing by the window. An energy pours off her, but I can't quite pinpoint what it is. There's a restlessness to it, mixed with a tension that makes the hairs on the back of my neck stand on end.

I'll fix whatever is worrying her. Anything to stop her from looking like that, as if the weight of the world is sitting on her chest. Christ, I'd fucking burn the world to the ground for her if it would make her feel better.

When her wide eyes meet mine, she comes to a stop and her body visibly relaxes. She crosses the room, meeting me halfway and clutching on to my shirt.

My eyes drop to her mouth, watching as she forms her words. "I have to tell you something," she rushes.

Bringing my hands up, I place them on either side of her head, smoothing my thumbs over her cheeks. I dip, ghosting my lips over hers before trailing across her jaw and over her neck. She tilts her head back, granting me greater access. "I'll fix it, but can it wait?"

"Massimo." My name is a breathless caress, a touch of admonishment trailing in its wake. The sound of it on her lips makes my cock impossibly hard.

"Say it again," I urge, my mouth tracing a path across her collarbone.

"Massimo, please," she moans when I cup her breast, massaging the full globe with my palm.

Hooking my hands into the neckline of her dress, I rip the material down the center.

Margot gasps, the sound music to my *fucking* ears. Finding her bare, I growl before taking her nipple into my mouth and sucking on it, flicking my tongue over the hardened point.

Grazing her nipple with my teeth, I suck the bud one final time before releasing it with a pop. When I straighten to my full height, I devour her with my eyes, reveling in the flush covering her chest and cheeks. *She's fucking beautiful*. I need her.

My voice comes out low, reverberating in my chest when I demand, "What do you need?"

Stepping into her space, I run my thumb over the pulsating vein in her throat, my gaze flicking between her hooded eyes and slightly parted lips.

She blinks up at me, lost in the evident desire between us but trying to fight her way through. Placing her hands on my chest, Margot blows out a breath. "I— God, I want you, but not right now."

My brow tugs down and I rest my hands over hers before demanding, "What's wrong?"

Stepping back and taking her warmth with her, she moves to the bed and picks up my T-shirt—the one she insists on wearing to bed—pulling it over her head and hiding her body from my view. "I can't have this conversation naked."

She perches on the end of the bed, tapping the spot next to her, but I don't move. My curiosity is piqued, but I'm not sitting down for whatever this is. "We are not getting a divorce," I grit out.

She shakes her head, wetting her lips but doesn't speak.

"What is it, Margot?" I demand, folding my arms over my chest.

"Who is Elio?" she asks, her voice quiet but the hint of anguish adds a slight tremor to it.

I narrow my eyes, my body tensing before I take an involuntary step forward. "Where did you hear that name?"

She bites down on her bottom lip, looking up at me from under her lashes. "I overheard a conversation. They mentioned three names." She ticks them off on her fingers. "Elio, Mattia and Francesco."

With every name, my muscles stiffen, until my entire body is rigid, and I grind out, "What did you overhear?"

Margot looks down at her lap, picking at her nail polish before returning to meet my gaze. Shaking her head, she replies, "I don't want to tell you if it's going to end how I think it will."

"And how do you think it will end?" I ask, injecting a reluctant softness into my tone.

She lifts her head, her eyes holding mine, something akin to regret, or perhaps sympathy, shining in the green depths. "You'll do what you need to do, I suppose."

Margot stands, closing the distance between us and wrapping her arms around my waist as she presses her head to my chest. Automatically, I lift my arms, wrapping them around her, offering her comfort. "I just don't want that on my conscience, but more than that, I don't want your death on it either."

I rest my chin on the top of her head, trying to reassure her when I say, "Whatever it is they've done, *they* have made that decision. Not you. You haven't forced them into this. They have to face the consequences. That isn't on you, Margot." Pulling her away from me, I bend my knees until we're eye-level. "Tell me what you overheard."

Her eyes search mine before she steps out of my hold completely. Walking to the window, she leans against the wall as she stares out into the gardens. Her voice is quiet when she finally speaks, the magnitude of what she is telling me dragging her down. "I was heading to the kitchen to hang out with Alma when I overheard someone on the phone to Elio. They were in the alcove near the main staircase."

Margot darts her eyes to me and I incline my head for

her to continue. We can talk about how she shouldn't put herself in dangerous situations later. "He was talking to Elio, telling him that he had everything in hand and that there wouldn't be any more problems because he's in charge of the investigation..."

I tune her out, my mind stuck on that small and possibly, to her at least, insignificant piece of information. I'm assaulted by a range of emotions, but the one that stands out the most is my fury, it battles with the betrayal until all I can feel is the fire burning in my veins.

"Who?" I bark.

Margot jumps, but in the midst of my anger, I can't comfort her.

She hesitates before whispering, "Aldo."

No. I want to tell her she's wrong, that he would never betray me, because betraying me would be like betraying my father. But the truth is, the second she said he'd told Elio he was investigating the case, I knew. I just needed her to confirm because I never would have thought he would do this.

Fuck.

Balling my fists, I squeeze until the muscles in my forearms burn from the tension. I spin toward the door, the room blurring around me. Rage thrums in my veins, barely leashed.

"Massimo, please. Don't do what I think you're going to do."

I stop with my hand on the doorknob, staring down at the metal ring on my finger. We both know that I have no choice. This is my duty, just like it is my duty to protect her. I cross the room back to Margot, pressing a kiss to her forehead, before sliding my ring off. When I place it in her palm, her fingers curl around it like it's something fragile. "I won't have his blood tainting my ring, look after it for me. He has to pay for what he's done."

Teary eyes hold mine when I step back. A single tear falls free, tumbling down her cheek and pooling on her chin. I cup her face with one hand, pressing my lips to hers before I step back. "His death isn't on your hands. *He did this*. The moment he colluded with our enemies was the moment he signed away his life." And I won't hesitate to take him out.

She nods, mumbling, "I don't like it, but I understand."

I stare at her for a moment before stepping away, in awe of the woman I married. She doesn't stop me this time but I don't miss the shaky breath she drags in. How can she have compassion for a man that could kill her in the blink of an eye?

The irony isn't lost on me that I could kill her, as I have many others before, and yet, she puts her faith in me to protect her. *To love her*.

Chapter 35

Massimo

Daniele is waiting for me in my office when I arrive, lounging on the couch and oblivious to the shitstorm I'm carrying in with me. My anger has only grown during the walk through the quiet corridors from the bedroom, and it's about to explode.

"I got your text. What's happened?" Daniele asks.

I settle into one of the armchairs across from him and pull out my phone. "There's been a development in the situation with the rat. I need to update both you and Leonardo."

Daniele nods, propping his ankle on his knee, unaware of the bomb I'm about to drop. With my phone on speaker, I set it on the table between us and listen as it rings.

"Boss," Leonardo answers on the second ring, his tone low.

"I have an update for you both." I pause, my mind

searching for the right words. "Margot has just informed me that she overheard a conversation between one of my men and Elio Moretti."

Daniele's brows pull low, and on the other end of the phone, Leonardo whistles. There's movement on the line before the background noise dies down. "Does she know who?" Leonardo asks.

I nod even though Leonardo can't see me. The weight of his name is heavy on my chest. "Yes. It's Aldo."

Leonardo scoffs. "The man that has worked for your family for longer than you have been alive is the rat?"

I pinch the bridge of my nose. "Yes."

"We've been misled before," Daniele says carefully. "How sure is she that it was him?"

I don't blame him for being cautious. We weren't when we believed Aurora to be involved in the attacks, and look how that ended.

"She overheard him telling Elio that he was investigating the case himself. Unless it was you she heard, there is only one person in this house *today* that it could be. Besides, she knew about Mattia, Elio, and Francesco."

"Fuck," Leonardo breathes.

"*Cazzo*," Daniele mutters.

They've got that right. The gravity of the situation isn't lost on us. We all know what comes next. After a betrayal, there is always death.

Leonardo's voice eventually cuts through the quiet. "It'll take me a couple of hours, but I'll be there before sunrise."

"No. We've got this." I meet Daniele's gaze. Having Leonardo here won't change the outcome, and besides, he has other lives depending on him now. "Look after Haven and I'll let you know when it's done."

He's quiet for a moment before replying, "Thank you, Massimo. I'm sorry I'm not there."

I disconnect the call. "Where did Callum get to with the cellphones? Aldo has clearly been using one to communicate outside of the house."

Daniele exhales, resting his elbow on the arm of the couch. "Last I checked, he'd gone through them all and found nothing, but if Aldo was using a burner, it wouldn't have covered the batch we gave to Callum. If he truly is the rat—"

Cutting him off, I say, "He is. She would not lie." That much I know for certain. Margot has been nothing but honest with me throughout our marriage.

He nods, before continuing, "We gave him full access to the investigation, so he could have steered it in any direction he saw fit."

We made a mistake bringing Aldo into the fold, but how could we have known? Aldo has been by my side since I took over. He was by my father's, and before that, he was by my nonno's. Hell, it was my nonno who took him under his wing when he was eighteen and this is what he does? It's almost inconceivable. *And yet I know it is a fact.*

Glancing at my watch, I make a note of the time. It's going to be the early hours of the morning for Romeo in

Palermo, but he needs to know. Picking up my phone, I type out a quick message.

MASSIMO

> We have found the rat. I am dealing with it. Will update once it's done.

Standing, I pocket my phone. "Bring him to the basement."

Chapter 36

Massimo

"You wanted to see me?" Aldo asks as he saunters into the room without a care in the fucking world and oblivious to the noose he's tied around his own neck.

Daniele follows him in, closing and locking the door behind them. I push away from the wall, adrenaline coursing through my veins now that the bastard is standing in front of me. The man conspiring to kill me and those I have a duty to protect.

With a calm I do not feel, I indicate to the chair in the middle of the room just behind where he's come to a stop. "Take a seat."

Aldo's brows lift, but only slightly, and I'm certain that he didn't mean for me to see. He smooths a hand over his tie and lifts his chin a fraction. "I think I'll stand."

I take a step toward him. "I wasn't giving you a choice."

His throat bobs in a nervous swallow. Even in the dingy lighting of the room, I can see his uncertainty. It's like a veil has been lifted, and where I once saw a strong and powerful man, I now only see a weak, greedy *rat*.

I take another step, and he takes one back, putting him in Daniele's reach. Clamping a hand onto his shoulder, Daniele forces Aldo into the chair, holding him steady.

He squirms, his eyes wide with panic. "What's going on?"

Brandishing a zip tie from my pocket, I grab one of his wrists, looping the tie around it before tying him to the chair. His heavy, panicked breathing is the only sound as I work on the other one and then move to his ankles.

"Massimo?" he calls when I step back, curiosity colliding with the worry in his expression. "This is unnecessary. I will tell you whatever you want to know."

Straightening, I tilt my head. "Is that so? Because I think you've had plenty of time to tell me your *secret*."

He barks a laugh, darting a glance at Daniele before returning his attention to me. "I have no secrets."

Liar. The corner of my mouth lifts in a sadistic smirk, and I shake my head before heading toward the countertop where a selection of tools are laid out. "How long have you been working with Elio Morretti?" I ask, catching his reaction over my shoulder.

Panic flits across his features before he shuts it down like the man my grandfather taught him to be. I select a hammer from the counter, the tool heavy in my hand and rusted from use. My arm falls to my side, laden down with the weapon as I turn and prowl toward him, waiting for an answer.

"I don't know what you're talking about. I haven't spoken to Elio Morretti in years. Not since your father was trying to negotiate with him."

Shaking my head, I line the hammer head up with his knee. "I have a reliable witness and she has told me otherwise."

Aldo's features transform, giving me a peek at the monster beneath the surface. "You mean that *bitch* of a wife you have? She's lucky."

I grind my teeth, forcing my tone to remain calm. "Yeah? How do you figure that?"

"The attempted kidnapping? That was Elio, he had plans for her. She'd have gotten what she deserved being the cheap whore she is. They'd have defiled and murdered her to get you to break. And like the weak man you are, you'd have done whatever it took to protect her," he snarls.

I swing the hammer into his knee. It hits with a sickening crunch, and his cries echo around the room. "Fucking call her a whore again," I snarl, spittle flying from my mouth and landing on his face.

Aldo gasps for air, his eyes brimming with hate. It's enough for my control to snap. I hurl the hammer aside and it clatters to the floor, but the sound barely penetrates the fog of fury wrapped around me. Grabbing the collar of his jacket, I bring my fist back and slam it into his face, over and over again, ignoring the pain that radiates from my knuckles.

A wildness runs through me, untamable and hungry for his blood. Daniele steps in, forcing me to take a step back. He stands between us as he holds my gaze. "We need answers," he reminds me.

We both know that Aldo won't tell us what we want to know. Like us, he has been trained to withstand whatever torture methods we might use, but it won't stop me trying to break him.

I suck in a breath, forcing the room back into focus and staring at Aldo's now bruised and bloody face. I've beaten men before, killed, tortured, and broken them. But this? This is the first time I've ever lost control.

We need to know what is coming next, undoubtedly something is, and the man in front of me is the only one who can give us an answer. Flipping out on him and letting my rage get the best of me can't happen again.

Shoving Daniele's hands away, I nod before stepping around him, my chest heaving. "Let's try this again, shall we." I pick up the pliers from the counter and crack my neck as I move toward Aldo. "Hold his hand steady," I instruct Daniele, who follows my command without question. Grabbing Aldo's pinkie, I slip the pliers under his nail. "How long have you been working with Elio Moretti?"

Aldo laughs, the sound dark and sinister. "You are wasting your time. There is nothing you can do to me—"

In one swift movement, I yank up, ripping his fingernail from the bed of his finger. Aldo screams, his voice raw before he gasps for air.

"Exactly how long do you think you will last? You know what I am capable of and where this is going."

"Just fucking do it," he snarls, pulling at the restraints.

I move to the next finger. "Where is Elio?"

Sweat beads on his temple. "Go to hell."

His body tenses, waiting for me to strike. I don't disappoint, pulling up and ripping off another nail, his screams tearing into the air.

We repeat the cycle—me asking a question, him refusing to answer until all of his fingernails have been removed. He's trembling, his chin sagging against his chest, but he hasn't broken and he probably never will.

Daniele clears his throat, forcing my focus to shift to him. When he nods toward Aldo's neck, he pulls at the collar. *Fedeltà Eterna*: Eternal Loyalty. The same tattoo we saw on the man who tried to kidnap Margot. *The one Elio's men get as their pledge.*

Shaking my head, I grab a fistful of Aldo's hair, yanking his head back. "It's over," I say. "Tell me why? Why betray me? My father and his father before him trusted you. They thought they had your loyalty. Betraying me is a betrayal of them. You know how this works."

His breath rattles. "They did have my loyalty." His

top lip curls, as he looks at me through bloodied, swollen, and bruised eyes.

"I gave everything to your family and when you stepped into your father's shoes, you all but retired me. The sacrifices I made were for nothing because you never gave me your loyalty in return," he snarls.

"You thought you would kill me and what? Take over my operations because you wanted a bigger piece of the pie? Get fucking real. Elio would have killed you as soon as you served your purpose."

Denial floods Aldo's gaze and he opens his mouth to speak but nothing comes out. I see the moment realization seeps into his eyes, quickly followed by regret. *Too fucking late.*

I walk to the counter on the far side of the room, picking up the knife I've used countless times and turning it over in my hand. The handle is heavy, but it's the sharpness of the blade that glints under the dim lighting which holds my attention.

"Do you know what the funny thing is?" I pause. "I looked up to you when I took over, but I guess it's true what my father said, 'power will rot a foundation from within and greed is insatiable, but the two together. Well, that's combustible and will ruin a man.'"

Standing behind him, I fist Aldo's hair, pulling it back until his neck is exposed and he's staring at the ceiling. I place the blade against his skin, pausing as memories flash through my mind. The one that stands out the most is from moments ago, the disgust on his face and the vile words he spoke about my wife.

Without another thought, I slide the blade across his throat. He releases a gurgled gasp, his body shuddering and his lips moving, yet no words come out. Our gazes lock, and I hold his until the life drains from him, and he goes limp in the chair. It's only then that I release him and step away. He was never going to win and as he took his last breath, he knew it.

A strange sense of grief washes over me as I walk from the cell without a word. I did what had to be done to protect my family and my men.

There is nobody else to blame for this except for Aldo and he paid the ultimate price. And yet, shame and guilt eat away at me for having allowed him to do what he did, right under my nose and for having to kill a man that my father and grandfather considered family.

Blowing out a breath, I pull my phone out and open the message thread with Romeo before adding Leonardo.

MASSIMO

It's done.

The two words hold a heaviness to them, but I brush it off and press send before shoving my phone back into my pocket. It's not really done, in the sense of having gotten rid of the threat, we still have to find Elio and take care of Anastasia but at least now, we can move forward without our every move being reported.

At the top of the basement stairs, I lift my hand to the

doorknob, my gaze focusing on the bruises forming on my skin. Hours ago, I was looking at my hand and the ring that represents loyalty, unity, but now all I see is an ugliness on my skin. It's a bitter reminder of what happened here tonight that will stay with me for the days to come.

As the reality of his death and betrayal sinks in, I let my feet guide me, my mind numb to everything but one thought. *I need to see her.* I need to know that I haven't drowned in the darkness and that there is something worth saving.

Margot is the only light I have in the shadows of my life and I want to keep her that way.

Chapter 37

Margot

Somewhere in the distance, a door creaks open, followed by footsteps echoing down the hall. My heart stutters, a painful reminder that the information I gave to Massimo hours ago, will have ended in a man's last breath. I exhale, waiting for him to return; to confirm what I already know is done.

The room is bathed in a soft glow from the moonlight that shines through the bedroom window. I've been watching the world outside continue to revolve, contemplating the 'what-ifs' of our situation. What if I hadn't told Massimo what I heard? Would Aldo have been able to follow through on his plan? Would I have been next? They're all questions that will remain unanswered, at least for me.

I feel him before I turn to see him. He halts in the middle of the room, his eyes unfocused and seeming to look through me, rather than at me. His black shirt bears darker patches and for a moment, I wonder what he was forced to do before I clear the thought from my mind. I want to go to him, to give him comfort, but I don't know if he'll let me.

He isn't the same man that left this room. I can feel the change in him, and I don't know how to get him back.

My attention skims down his body, making sure he's at least physically okay, even if I can feel his pain down to my very core.

When my attention lands on his hands, he holds them up, staring at them as if for the first time. Something about the sight of them sets him in motion. He turns, and without a word, walks into the bathroom, closing the door softly behind him.

Nausea grips my stomach and I force myself to take steadying breaths. This isn't because of what Massimo has done, this is because of what could have happened. I'm glad that I told him what I'd uncovered, even if that means he had to kill a man. *I don't know what I would have done if I'd lost him.*

Unsure of what do to, I wait. I don't know how much time passes, but I hear the shower running and then switching off. And when he returns to the bedroom, our gazes clash in the reflection of the window before he rips his away. The towel he has on is slung low on his hips and droplets of water fall from his hair, running down his chest. Fixated on him, I watch as he walks to the bed before taking a seat at the end.

"Come here." His voice is quiet but still strong and that provides me with some comfort.

Pushing away from the wall, I walk toward him, coming to a stop in front of his parted legs. He grabs the T-shirt I threw on over my ripped dress earlier and pulls me into him, burying his nose in my chest as he sucks in a heavy breath. I wrap my arms around his head, holding him close, the faint hum of the air conditioner the only sound around us.

Massimo smooths his hands up the back of my thighs, applying a light pressure that forces my knees to buckle onto the bed. I straddle his lap as his hands find their way under the cotton T-shirt.

With his nose stroking the column of my neck, he murmurs, "I need you."

I dive my fingers into his hair and hold him still as I lean back. "I'm here," I whisper.

The evidence of Aldo's betrayal has clearly taken its toll on him. He's broken, something I never thought I'd see. He needs me to mend the pieces of him that have shattered at the truth he's had to face, and as his wife, I will do exactly that.

With my eyes searching his, I try to tell him how much he's come to mean to me, that I'm sorry for what he had to do but that I love him anyway.

I love him.

The thought hits me like a bullet straight to the chest. But I don't have time to process it before his mouth is on mine. His kiss is searing yet tender as he coaxes my mouth open. He's seeking solace and I give it to him freely.

When Massimo stands, I wrap my legs around his waist, our mouths still fused as our tongues tease and tangle. He turns us, climbing over the bed before lowering me onto the mattress.

Settling between my legs, he breaks the kiss, trailing his hot mouth from my lips, over my jaw and down my neck. My skin pebbles in his wake and my nipples pucker in anticipation. I *want* him. I *need* him. More than the air I need to survive. I'm too lost in the haze of *us* to figure out why that is, or what it means, but I will. *Later.*

He sits up, his towel long gone as he kneels over me looking like a God in all his nakedness.

"Take it off, I want to see my wife," he commands, the look in his eyes heating every inch of my skin.

Sitting up, I pull the cotton material over my head before throwing it on the floor and turning my attention to the ruined dress. My chest heaves, every breath fueled with an excitement that I can't control. My fingers fumble with the material before I free myself and throw the dress in the same direction as the T-shirt.

Suddenly shy, I dart a glance at Massimo. It doesn't escape me that this is the first time my husband has seen me fully naked.

What if he doesn't like what he sees?

I shake off the thought, my focus moving down his body, over his hard abs to his cock. It's thick and jutting out from his body with pre-cum leaking from the tip. I lick my lips, swallowing down the saliva pooling in my mouth.

I reach out, wrapping my hand around him. Rubbing my thumb over the tip, I look up at him. His face is tense and he hisses, placing his hand over mine and guiding me up and down his shaft before removing my hand completely.

Easing me back onto the mattress, he hovers above me, his cock resting on my pussy. I cup his face, my focus shifting momentarily to his ring on my thumb before returning to his eyes.

"I..." Emotion blocks my words from coming out. The weight of what he's had to do sitting heavy on my chest, because I know the gravity of the situation. "I'm sorry you had to do that."

Sliding my hand between us, I wrap my hand around Massimo's cock, stroking his length. He grazes his teeth over one nipple, as he rolls the other between his thumb and forefinger. The pleasure and pain that rush through me has my back arching, pushing my chest further into his face, and silently begging for more.

Massimo sucks the tight bud into his mouth, sliding his tongue around it before releasing it with a pop. He moans, a deep guttural sound as I stroke him, squeezing the head of his cock before running my thumb over the slit. Moisture floods my pussy and my body aches to ease his pain.

Massimo groans, burying his face in the crook of my neck as he pushes inside of me in one smooth stroke. My walls clench around him, my slickness helping him to slide to the hilt with ease.

"Fuck. You're so wet," he breathes, his teeth nipping at my skin.

I wrap my legs around his waist, holding him tight as tremors ripple through my body. Massimo pulls back, his gaze searching mine. My lips part and my breaths come in short, gasping pants, mirroring his own. *I feel like I've run a marathon.*

Hooking my leg over his arm, Massimo pulls back slightly before thrusting forward, his pace slow and deliberate. I pull in a shuddering breath, the intensity in the air almost suffocating.

Something about this feels so different from any other time we've been together. This isn't about ownership, power, or dominance. This is about him needing me to make him *whole.*

Through half-lidded eyes, I commit every inch of his face to memory from the thick vein in his neck to the raw emotion flitting through his eyes that I can't quite name.

He keeps his rhythm slow, yet relentless, building my orgasm from nothing to a symphony in a matter of minutes. My walls pulsate around him, pulling his release from him as my own explodes. Black dots fill my vision but I can't break the hold his gaze has on me as it shudders through me. Our moans collide, raw and unguarded.

He collapses on top of me, panting before he pulls out and rolls to my side. My hand finds his as I stare at the ceiling. Our fingers lock and I glance at him to see his eyes closed and his chest rising and falling in heaving breaths.

Lifting his hand, I press a kiss to his bruised knuckles before sliding his ring from my thumb onto his ring finger, reclaiming him as *mine*.

Chapter 38

Margot

After the events of last night, the house feels different, like it can finally breathe. I might not have been around when all this mess started, but even *I* have a lightness in my step—a near giddiness. I guess that's what happens when you realize you're in love.

It blows my mind that I've fallen for the man who forced me into this marriage, who tore me from everything I knew. But looking back and seeing how far we have come, even in such a short space of time, I wouldn't change a thing.

I dart down the corridor that leads to Massimo's office. His door is open ahead of me and a smile that I can't contain pulls at the corners of my mouth. As I approach, voices drift out and my heart skips a beat. I keep going, picturing the look on Massimo's face when he sees me.

I've visited him in his office a few times over the last few days, and each time, we've been consumed by each other. Our mouths always collide before we've barely said our first words.

When I reach for the doorknob, I freeze, my hand hovering in midair at the sound of voices on the other side. I listen intently, my curiosity getting the better of me.

"Something needs to change, Massimo. I told Luigi and I'll tell you; your wife is a distraction. You need to get her in line before you draw more attention to yourself. I am aware of what happened at Aces with your soldier, and then for you to leave our dinner in the manner that you did."

Antonio.

I've only met him once and even then it wasn't *my* behavior that needed questioning. Yes, I pushed Massimo, but I was certain nobody else was aware of my mood.

I listen, waiting for Massimo to defend me, to tell him that he's wrong, or to mind his own business.

"I know." Massimo sighs, like I'm a burden that he knows he must deal with.

I stumble back, my jaw going slack. Everything that I thought we had burns to ashes around me with those two little words. I thought we'd found peace, that we could make this marriage work, and that after last night, maybe he felt the same way I do. *Was it all a ploy to...* God, I don't even know what he would hope to achieve by using me.

Tears prick my eyes before movement on the other side of the door has me rushing back the way I came. *I need a plan.* To put my armor in place so that he can't manipulate me with sex to get his own way. In fact, I won't let him touch me ever again. I can't believe I fell for him, that I thought we had a future.

Within minutes, I push through the door into our bedroom. The bed is still unmade from our morning sex and I slap a hand over my mouth to muffle the sob that weaves its way up my throat and spills from my lips.

How could I have been so stupid? To think that a man in his position could feel anything close to an emotion such as love is laughable. But what's worse is that I love him.

Well, not anymore.

Now, I'm no longer suffocated by the fog of my delusions. I can see everything so clearly. I thought I mattered to him. *How could I have been so wrong?*

Stalking into the closet, I pull out a duffel bag, throwing things into it without really looking. My vision blurs and I force myself to stop, staring at the ceiling. *I will not cry.* Not over a man that should *never* have meant anything to me in the first place. Ethan deserved my tears. He did nothing but love me unconditionally. Massimo, well, he deserves my wrath.

Sniffing away the hurt and allowing my anger to seep in, I stare down at what I've packed before tipping it all back out. *I'm not taking a single thing he's given me.* He can burn them for all I care.

Footsteps in the bedroom raise the hairs on the back of my neck, and I stand, sweeping the mess I've made on the floor out of sight under the bench in the middle of the room. The closet door opens, and Massimo stands on the threshold.

"Want to join me for lunch? Alma said she would set us up in the garden as it's not raining and there's no forecast."

I glare at him, my anger bubbling beneath the surface. *No.* I'm not just angry, I'm furious. At him but more importantly at myself. I let him make me feel *safe*.

Without thinking, I curl my top lip in disgust and spit, "I wouldn't have lunch with you if you were the last man on Earth." His brows tug low. Inhaling, I snarl, "I want a divorce."

Massimo pushes away from the doorjamb, a dangerous glint in his eyes. A muscle in his jaw flexes, the only sign of his own anger as he prowls toward me.

"Don't you dare touch me." My voice trembles, betraying me at the same time as moisture pools in my eyes. "I heard you talking to Antonio about how much you need to get me in line."

He halts, his features transforming and a mask sliding down, hiding the darkness from me. I realize now that I don't know this man, not really.

Folding his arms over his chest, Massimo blocks the only exit, and for a moment, I wish I'd had the forethought to confront him somewhere else, somewhere where I could run from him.

He lets out a short, bitter laugh. "I suppose I only have myself to blame for not setting you straight about eavesdropping, but in this case, it might have helped if you'd stuck around for the *whole* conversation."

He's annoyed that I've overheard his conversation? *The bastard.* He doesn't get to be mad at me when I haven't done anything wrong.

My anger erupts, consuming me like a fire and burning any sense of self-preservation I had as I scream, "I shouldn't have been a topic of conversation. *Full stop.* I am your wife."

Pacing, I scrub my hands over my face in an attempt to calm myself. It's only when I'm sure I can sound like a reasonable adult that I speak again. "Our entire relationship has been built on the foundation of you getting whatever you want, and I'm tired of conforming to your wishes. If you give me nothing else, give me this. I *want* a divorce, Massimo."

A muscle ticks in his jaw as he regards me. Stuffing his hands into his pockets, he replies, "If that is what you want, then I will give you your divorce." Elation crashes into me, my entire body relaxing before he adds, "If you win."

My brows pull low and I wrap my arms around my waist before I catch myself and drop them to my side. "What do you mean?"

Whatever he says next, I know that I'm going to have

to have my wits about me. Massimo is a smart man, and I wouldn't put it past him to fix whatever it is so that he wins. He bares his teeth in some semblance of a smile, but I can't help feeling like I'm Red Riding Hood walking straight into the wolf's trap.

"We play a hand of poker. You win and I'll have the divorce papers drawn up and signed for you by morning. But if I win, we remain married." He prowls toward me, coming to a stop when he's inches away. "You will give me all of you." He runs a hand down my chest, stopping over my heart. There isn't a chance that he can't feel the erratic beat as it pounds. "*Every* last part."

Stepping back, I put some distance between us, lifting my chin as I reply, "Fine. But I won't let you win. You'll never have me again." *Even if I don't know how to play poker.*

With a chuckle, he leans in close. "We'll see."

Chapter 39

Margot

I stare at the cards in my hand, trying to figure out if they're any good. A ten of diamonds and an ace of clubs—what the hell am I even supposed to do with that? I don't know why I agreed to this. *Because you're desperate.*

How am I supposed to win against a guy who plays poker on a weekly basis when I've not touched a pack of cards since I was a kid? I'm going to lose, and then I'll be stuck married to a man who thinks it's his right to mold me into the perfect wife. *This was a ridiculous idea.*

Massimo lays the first three cards down on the coffee table between us. He's sitting on the couch with a glass of whiskey in front of him and I'm on a cushion on the floor, my glass of wine untouched.

I stare at the cards I've been dealt, wracking my brain for the information I crammed this afternoon, but there was so much to take in that I don't think I've actually retained any. A jack of hearts, a seven of clubs, and a queen of diamonds sit on the table before me. I have no idea if this is good or bad.

"You want to know what I told him?" Massimo asks, everything about him cool, calm and collected. The polar opposite to the panic and uncertainty that I'm feeling.

I sip my drink if only to give myself something to do. Keeping my eyes on my cards, I murmur, "No. It doesn't matter, Massimo. None of this does." *Liar*.

In my peripheral, I see him nod. "You're right." Massimo moves in his seat, casually tossing a chip into the middle of the table. "Raise you five."

Crap. He's betting more. That means he's confident, right? Or is he bluffing? I have no idea how to tell. I peek up at him under my lashes. His expression is unreadable, the very definition of a poker face.

I eye the chip he's just thrown in, contemplating my next move. I don't want to fold, but I don't know if I *should* fold. *I don't remember the rules.* Do they even apply in a game like this, where it's just the two of us and we have no dealer?

Deciding not to overthink it, I grab one of my chips with the number five on it and drop it into the pile. It lands with a soft clink against his. His stare is heavy and assessing, like he's reading every nervous twitch of my fingers.

He smirks. "You're supposed to say, *call*."

Rolling my eyes, I huff, "Call."

He deals the next card. It's another face card—this

time the king of spades. My stomach tightens. There's a king, queen, and jack now. Does it matter that they aren't the same suit? What does the ace count as? I rub at my temple, trying to ease the ache that's forming. It's going to take a miracle for me to win at this point.

Sliding a chip between his fingers, he tosses it onto the pile. "Raise you five."

This is it, with this next card, I'll know my fate. Blowing out a breath, I throw in a chip and ask, "What did Alvin owe you?"

Massimo freezes, before shaking it off and reaching for the deck. Tension fills the space between us, and I wonder if he'll answer me, if he'll tell me my worth. *I should have asked sooner*.

"Half a million."

"Dollars?" My eyes widen. *I'm speechless*. That's a huge sum. It might not be much to Massimo, but to me and the people in *my* world, it's astronomical. Was Josephine aware of just how much trouble Alvin was in?

"Yes, five hundred thousand dollars."

When I don't respond, Massimo slides the final card from the top of the deck before placing it on the table. I watch as he flips it over, my throat tightening, making it difficult to swallow. *Ace of hearts*. The irony of the card isn't lost on me. He has my heart, he probably always will, no matter how much I wish he didn't.

I throw my hand down, leaning back against the couch. "Did I win?"

We stare at each other for an eternity before he drops

his gaze to the cards. He takes a breath, one that feels heavier than it should, before he exhales a quiet laugh. "Yeah," he murmurs. "You did."

"I did?" I can't keep the shock from my voice as I stare at my cards.

"Yeah." His voice is quieter this time, almost resigned. He lays his cards out in front of us. "You got a straight, which beats my three-of-a-kind."

Why does it feel like a weight is sitting on my chest? It feels impossible to breathe, or talk, or do anything but stare at him. I should be happy that I won, but all I feel is my heartache.

Massimo knocks his fingers on the tabletop. *Once. Twice.* The rhythmic tap is steady and measured, but his jaw tightens, showing a sliver of emotion. He shakes his head, like he's shaking off a thought, then stands. "As promised, you have your freedom."

Our eyes meet, something swimming in the depths of his that I'm certain mirrors my own.

Regret.

I just don't know if it's because he's lost me or that he had me in the first place.

"I told Antonio that you drive me insane, but if anything, it's made me a better man. I told him that I like the push and pull that we have, that you will stand up for yourself and call me out on my shit. But most of all, I like the fact that you aren't tainted by the gore of our world. I told him that I wouldn't change a thing about you or make you conform in any way," Massimo says, before huffing out a breath and shaking his head once more. "If you'd stuck around, you would've heard *that*."

And then he walks away, leaving me to come to terms with the loss of him and his truth hanging over me.

Isn't this what I wanted? Yes and no.

Why do I feel so bereft? I blink back tears that I won't let fall. Not here anyway.

It's over.

We're over.

But I don't want us to be.

The silence that surrounds me is deafening. I press my hand to my chest, trying to ease the ache, but it's no good. It's there, deep and raw. I'm not sure it will ever go away.

This is the end of our marriage.

I demanded it, but now I'm not sure I want it at all.

Chapter 40

Massimo

Margot appears at the top of the stairs, a duffel bag in hand and a forlorn look on her face that I'm certain matches my own. *I didn't think she'd really leave.* Not after I told her what I said to Antonio. But I guess it's too little, too late.

When she reaches the bottom step, her gaze lifts to mine before it falls away and she crosses the distance between us. Her face is a perfectly painted mask when she comes to a stop in front of me, dropping the bag at her feet.

An ache settles in my chest as my eyes search her red-rimmed ones. *She's been crying?* Because she doesn't want to go or because she can't believe she's finally free?

"Could you arrange for someone to drive me to the city?" she asks, her voice quiet and nothing like the woman I married.

I work my jaw, overcome with emotions I can't quite identify. "Daniele will take you. Where are you going?"

She looks at the floor, her shoulders dropping as she sighs heavily. "To Josephine's, for now at least. But I won't stay there for long, given... everything."

Will she go back to Ethan?

The question hits me like a sucker punch, robbing the air from my lungs. I know that I can't stop her, but he's no good for her. *She belongs with me.*

A door opens somewhere at the back of the house, and without thinking, I take hold of her arm and pull her into the living room. *Nobody else needs to witness this.*

I kick the door shut behind us and we're blanketed in a vacuum of silence.

My gaze shifts to the table behind her, the one we sat at mere moments ago. The one that ended our marriage. *No, I ended our marriage.* A stupid game that I thought I'd win but really I left our future up to chance and I fucking lost.

Margot turns, walking to stand at the back of the couch before huffing out a shaky breath and lifting her head to the ceiling. I want to beg her to stay, but what would be the use? She'd only tell me no, because if that was what she wanted, she never would have packed her bag. *She wouldn't be leaving.*

With only my instinct to guide me, I cross the room, standing behind her and wrapping my arms around her waist. I drop my forehead to her shoulder and breathe in her sweet scent.

If this is it, I need to feel her one last time. To imprint the memory of her onto my skin. I need something I can hold on to in the dark hours when I long for her.

I dust my lips over her shoulder and she angles her head away from me, exposing the smooth column of her throat. *This is the beginning of the end for us.*

Closing my eyes, I squeeze her tighter before smoothing my hand over her stomach and down the front of her thigh. She places her hand over mine. I expect her to pull it away, but instead, she guides it under her skirt and to the cotton covered mound of her pussy.

"Massimo," she whimpers.

The urge to beg her not to go hums inside of me, but the words won't come out. Instead, as her wetness soaks the material of her panties, I slide my hand to cup her breast, massaging it along with her clit.

My cock throbs in the confines of my pants, painfully hard and desperate to feel her wrapped around it. *One last time.* I don't want to rush this, but I need her like I need my next breath. *How am I going to survive when she's gone?*

"Margot," I groan when she arches her back and presses her ass against my erection.

I slip my hand into her panties, my fingers seeking out the swollen nub of her clit and applying a light pressure. Almost immediately, her hips buck; her silent plea for more. She's drenched, so I slide two fingers into her tight pussy, pressing my palm to her clit. She convulses around me, riding my hand, taking what she needs.

A strangled cry tears from her as she stiffens, her orgasm sounding almost painful. Light spasms wrack through her body, and while she's still riding the wave of her climax, I free my aching cock.

Pre-cum beads at the tip, running down the slit and dripping to the floor. I don't care about the mess, my only thought is burying myself in her one last time.

Removing my hand from her panties, I fist the fabric and move it to the side, sliding my cock through her slick folds before lining up my head with her entrance.

Pressing forward, I grit my teeth as her body envelops me. *Fuck.* Margot moans, indecipherable words spilling from her lips as her fingers grip the back of the couch. Our labored breaths mingle in the air.

Somewhere in the distance, I can hear a motor running, before I pull back and then thrust forward, losing myself in how well we fit together until it's all I can focus on.

Picking up my pace, I fall victim to my desperation, my movements jerky and uncoordinated as I search for my release. "Tell me you hate me," I command.

She doesn't say anything, so I lift the hem of her dress higher, fisting it in one hand as I smack her ass with the other. Margot cries out, her cheek almost instantly turning the most perfect shade of red.

Fuck, it's hard to think.

"Tell me you fucking hate me," I rasp.

Breathlessly, she gasps, "No."

God. I need her to tell me that she does. That is the

only explanation for why she's leaving me. I love her and she's fucking leaving me. *I love her.* The realization rips my heart from my chest. "Fucking say it, Margot—" My voice breaks on the words, even as I spill my cum inside of her one last time.

"I don't hate you," she cries out as she quivers around me, her body going tense. She convulses and covers her mouth with her hand before releasing a sob.

She doesn't hate me.

If she did, maybe letting her go wouldn't feel like I'd taken a bullet to the chest. Her head falls forward and I pull out of her, tucking myself back in before I straighten her panties and drop her dress back into place.

What we just did doesn't feel like goodbye. It felt like our souls entwined. I thought that the attacks on my family were going to be my biggest fight, but surviving Margot? That might just kill me.

I can't watch her leave. I can't be here as she walks out of the door, never to return.

Resting my hands on her hips, I hold her still, refusing to let her see me when I say, "I'll have the papers couriered to Josephine's house."

Margot nods, not looking up.

I want to tell her to stay. I want to beg her not to walk away. But I don't. *No, I can't.*

I'm Massimo *fucking* Marino, and I don't beg.

So instead, I walk away, the warmth of her already starting to fade from my life.

Chapter 11

Massimo

I *did the right thing.*

At least that's what I told myself when I signed the divorce papers the lawyer sent over.

I had no other choice.

That's what I said to convince myself that sending them to her was the right thing to do.

But now, as I sit here, staring at the empty space in front of me, I *know* that I made a colossal fucking mistake.

The phone on my desk rings, but I don't pick it up. I don't know how much time has passed since I entered my office. *Since she left me.* It feels like she took my existence with her and now all I'm left with is the faint scent of her that clings to my skin.

The call cuts off but within seconds it starts to ring again. Fucking hell, do I not have a house full of staff that are capable of answering a goddamn phone? Snatching up the handset, I bark, "What?"

"It's good to hear from you too, cousin," Romeo drawls, as if amused.

I slam the phone back into the cradle. It rings almost immediately, the sound shrill and grating on my senses.

Ring.

Ring.

Ring.

Exasperated, I pick up the phone and snap, "I have some shit going on here and I'm not in the mood for whatever you've called about."

I hear the squeak of Rome's chair on the other end of the line. His tone is low and serious when he says, "One, *do not* hang up on me again. I don't give a shit what you've got going on, you show me some respect. Two, what's happened? Another attack?"

Pinching the bridge of my nose, I reply, "Forgive me. No, there haven't been any new attacks. Not yet at least, but that would just be the cherry on top of my day."

"So, what's happened?" he urges, and I picture him leaning back in his chair.

I blow out a breath, staring out the window at the hills in the distance. A fog rolls over them, an indication of the early morning hour and the time she's been gone.

"Margot left me." Just speaking the words douses me in my failure. As a mafia don. But more importantly, as a husband.

"Will she come back?" Rome asks, matter-of-factly.

I can't hold back my bitter laugh. "Not a chance. She asked for a divorce so I played her for it and she won."

"I'm sorry, you played your wife for a divorce?" His confusion is evident and it's not a language barrier.

I've been so fucking idiotic.

Why did I think playing poker with her was the way to fix the problem? I should have just talked to her, but... "I didn't think she'd fucking win," I snap.

"What's that saying?" Romeo pauses. "Ah, yes, play stupid games, win stupid prizes? That's the one, right?"

I grind my jaw to the point of pain and grit out, "I mean this in the most respectful way possible, but *fuck you.*"

Romeo lets out a hearty chuckle, one that only a family member could get away with. I pull the phone away from my ear to stare at the handset. If I hang up on him again, what are the chances of him actually doing anything about it? Given we're family and he's thousands of miles away, it's got to be slim.

The line goes quiet and I press it back to my ear just in time to hear him ask, "Do you love her?"

"Yes." My answer is almost instantaneous. If there is only one thing I am ever certain of in my life, it is that I love Margot with every fiber of my being and I'm not ashamed to admit that.

"So go and get her back." He makes it sound so simple.

"I sent the divorce papers." There's a note of finality in my voice that I wish wasn't there.

"And?" Romeo asks, the word hanging between us heavy and accusatory.

"And that's the end," I bite.

Romeo sighs. "Massimo, if there is one thing I know about you, it's that you are clever, calculated, and unstoppable when you want something. It is how you got your nickname, right?" *The Crow*. "So, either you don't want her as much as you claim, or I was wrong about you. And I'm never wrong about people."

I let his words sink in. He's right about me, I am smart, calculated and don't give up on things I want. It's how I got Margot in the first place. *So why did I let her leave?*

The back of my eyes burn as I rest my head on my chair. I let her go because I wanted her to be happy. To not feel like she didn't have a choice. I've been clipping her wings for the entirety of our short marriage. I just figured if I let her go, she'd realize she wanted to stay.

Standing, my chair rolls back, hitting the cabinet behind me. "I have to go." *I have to win my wife back.*

"That's what I thought." I can hear the smile in Romeo's voice.

Before I disconnect the call, I ask, "How did you win Aurora back?"

He huffs out a laugh. "Truthfully, I don't know. I should have been on my knees begging for her forgiveness from the second we found her but I tried to give her space to recover. And when I realized that she might never forgive me, I told her she could leave. By the grace of God, she told me she couldn't, that she loved me and I was what she wanted. Don't get me wrong, afterward, I made it up to her in our own way, but I had to lay it all on the line before I could do that."

Nodding, I work through all of the different scenarios in my mind, trying to come up with a plan that will bring her home where she belongs.

I've spent my entire adult life making people do as I have commanded, no matter the consequences. But with Margot? If I truly love her—which I do—I shouldn't have let her go, I should have fought for her. I should have told her how I felt, so she had all of the facts.

"Listen, Massimo, don't overthink it. I bet you haven't even told her you love her, am I right?"

Scrubbing a hand over my jaw, I reply, "No, I haven't."

"So start there and see what she has to say. Look, I will call tomorrow and we can talk about the search for Anastasia."

"Okay," I reply distractedly.

"*Ciao.*"

Romeo disconnects the call and I stalk from my office with a newfound purpose. First, I need to find Margot and beg her to hear me out. And after that? Then I'll do whatever it fucking takes to bring her back home. *Where she belongs.*

Chapter 2

How do you survive missing someone who felt like they were a part of your existence?

I've cried countless tears and the heavy ache that presses down on my chest is making it hard to breathe. *I feel like a ghost.* And being in my old room hasn't provided me any comfort.

Things are awkward with Josephine and Alvin. He's hardly here and Josephine has taken to hovering by my door, trying to coddle me. I guess that's her way of trying to apologize, but all I can think about is *him. Massimo.*

There's no scent of him clinging to the sheets. No low murmur of his voice from down the hall. No weight of his presence filling the space like something tangible, something inescapable.

I need to get out of here.

Smoothing my palms down the front of my jeans, I force my body into motion, desperate to escape the suffocating air. I rush through the back door, following the path around the house to the front, my vision blurry as I gasp for air.

God, I wish that I wasn't so drowned in him. It feels like he's in my bloodstream, tangled in every part of me and there is nothing I can do to rid myself of him. *Even if I wanted to.*

A whimpered sob slips from my lips as the tears tumble unchecked down my cheeks. I swipe angrily at my eyes, frustrated that I feel so weak.

When I round the corner, I come up short, my brows pulling low. Leaning against his Bugatti parked at the curb, with his hands in his pockets and his dark eyes locked on me is my *husband*, Massimo.

My stomach tightens. Why is he here? To pick up the divorce papers? I haven't signed them. I couldn't bring myself to. Besides, they're stained with my tears and I couldn't bear for him to see that.

I sniff back my emotions, praying that he wasn't watching when I came around the corner. The last time he waited for me like this, I hated him. I'd felt trapped and forced into a fate that I couldn't escape from. But now? I'd give anything to have him take me home and return the love I feel for him. *I made a mistake by leaving.* Having him close, even if he didn't return my love, would have been preferential to *this*.

His face is a mask but as I get closer I see a flicker of vulnerability. *That can't be right.* "What are you doing here, Massimo?"

A muscle ticks in his jaw. "You know what."

My stomach twists. "I haven't signed the papers yet. Could you not give me more than a day to process the end of our marriage?" My voice cracks, betraying me. I force myself to look away, but I already know it's too late. The silence between us stretches heavy and thick.

"Fuck," he breathes, closing the space between us, stopping just short of touching me. "I didn't come here to get the fucking papers, Margot. I came to get *my wife*."

What? Does he want me now that I'm out of reach? "Why? Do you want me now that you can't have me? Am I just another shiny object to collect?" My voice wavers with anger and heartbreak.

"No. It was never like that."

I lift my eyes to his, searching the almost inky black depths. There's a raw longing, like he'd do anything to keep me, and my heart flutters with hope.

"I—You..." I stutter, unsure of what to say.

Massimo looks away, inhaling sharply before returning his focus to me. "Let me start again." He licks his lips, before clearing his throat. "From the moment I was shown your picture, I thought you were the most beautiful woman I'd ever laid eyes on. But when I met you and I saw the fight you had inside of you, I was obsessed. I'd planned for us to have a long engagement and find out if we were a good fit but the second you walked around that corner." He points in the direction I'd just come. "I knew I couldn't wait. There was just one thing I wanted to change about you."

My breath hitches, and I lean in a fraction, my heart pounding. "One thing?"

Smoothing back a strand of my hair, he draws his finger down my face, my neck, over my pounding heart and down my arm until he captures my hand. He lifts it between us, turning it over and watching the diamond that I couldn't bring myself to remove, glisten under the sun.

"Your last name. Fuck, that sounds corny." He laughs before falling serious again. "That need festered deep inside of me until claiming you was the only thing I could think about. I didn't care whether you wanted it or not. I guess I was living up to my nickname, taking what I wanted."

Oh.

All of the air leaves my lungs in a sharp exhale and I blink up at him. I swallow down my giddiness as everything starts to make sense. The fights. The passion. The way we've never stopped pulling toward each other, even when we were at war. He was drowning in us as much as I was.

Massimo places my hand over his heart and through the fabric of his shirt and I can feel its erratic beat. He closes his eyes and inhales deeply before opening them again, his sincerity and adoration for me shining brightly in his gaze. His lips part, but no sound comes out before he closes it and I watch his throat work.

When he finally speaks, his voice is a hushed confession, only meant for my ears. "I love you, Margot."

Holy shit. He loves me. I spent so long convincing myself that he never would, that our relationship was purely transactional. A way for him to possess me.

I suck in a breath, tears of joy filling my eyes as my face splits into a grin. This isn't him trying to manipulate me or win a game. This is him giving me everything he has and asking for all of me in return.

Throwing myself at him, I wrap my arms around his neck and bury my nose in the crook, inhaling his woodsy scent. *I love him so much it terrifies me.*

When I pull away, I smooth my fingers down his face and say, "I love you too, Massimo." Relief floods his expression. "Now, take me home."

His exhale is shaky before he threads his fingers into my hair and kisses me with so much passion and love that my knees buckle. Breaking away, he leads me to the car.

To our future.

Epilogue

Massimo

Six Months Later

Margot shuffles the deck, cards falling out and landing on the table. She's a goddamn amateur but she's got some killer good luck. Her fingers slip against the cards, but she's determined, sinking her teeth into her bottom lip as she concentrates.

"You're holding them all wrong, that's why you have no control over them," I murmur, smirking when she glares at me.

"You're supposed to be teaching me, not making fun of me," she huffs, but the way the corner of her mouth twitches tells me she's not serious.

I lean back in my chair, watching her struggle with a kind of satisfaction I should probably be ashamed of. She has no idea how much I enjoy watching her work through a challenge, refusing to back down. It reminds me of the beginning of our marriage and how she challenged me at every turn. She still does from time to time.

I reach across the table and pry the cards from her hands, my fingers brushing against hers. "Come here," I command, patting the couch cushion beside me.

She stands, straightening her silk bathrobe before walking around the table. I expect her to sit next to me, but she lifts a knee, straddling my lap.

I ignore the way my cock twitches as her warmth settles over me. This morning, she confessed how sore she was and so I am refusing to satisfy my needs. Hers will always come first.

"Lesson one is about control," I tell her, placing the cards in her hand and adjusting her grip. "If you look like you don't know what you're doing, people will eat you alive."

She uses her free hand to run a finger down my chest, and I bite the inside of my cheek. "People like you, you mean?"

I grin, holding her gaze and sitting up to dust my lips over the pulse beating at the base of her throat. "Especially people like me," I growl.

She tips her head back, bucking her hips against me before I pull away and she huffs out a breath. Folding her arms over her chest, she pouts. "I should have kept my mouth shut."

Shaking my head, I reply, "You should never keep something like that from me. If you're hurting, I want to know."

We fall quiet, a silent battle of wills taking place as we hold each other's gaze. She knows I'm right.

Margot drops her attention to the cards in her hand, holding them up between us before she looks me in the eye. "Are we actually going to play, or do you plan on giving me a lecture on how to shuffle cards first?"

The corner of my mouth twitches, and I tap her hip, indicating for her to move. It took some time, but we've taken the game that nearly ruined us and used it to rebuild our foundations.

"Let's play."

I deal the first hand out onto the coffee table as she walks back to her side. The lapels of her robe fall open, teasing me with a sliver of her breast. She picks up her cards, and I shift my attention to her face. Her expression changes, revealing just the slightest hint of *something* before she schools her features.

"You have a tell," I say, tossing a chip into the center.

She looks up at me, her fingers tightening on her cards. "What?"

I tap my fingers against the table, the corner of my mouth lifting in a smirk. "You hesitate when you get a good hand."

Margot tenses, and my chest blooms with pride when I see the determination that I love so much about her flow through her body. She adjusts in her seat, gripping her cards with more confidence. "I do not. I hesitate because I don't know what I'm doing."

I bark out a laugh. "If you say so."

She narrows her eyes. "I do. But let's say it was a tell, how do I fix it?"

I lean forward, resting my elbows on my knees. "You lie to yourself until you're convinced you have a dud hand."

Her mouth falls open slightly, and she scoffs. "That's it? Pretend my cards are bad?"

"That's it." I shrug.

"Okay," she calls, eyes locked on mine as I flip the next card.

She might be playing to win at poker, but I've already won. *Having her*. Calling her my wife. Knowing that she's mine—completely, irrevocably. That's the only victory that has ever truly mattered.

The End

Links to leave your review, pick up bonus content and to find the next book, can be accessed here:

Acknowledgments

First and foremost, I want to extend a huge thank you to my beta readers. Your energy and love for my characters in this new world continues to be inspiring.

Thank you to Jo-Ann for all of your check-ins, especially during my final read through of Marino. I appreciate you more than words can express!

Thank you to Sarah from Word Emporium for your thorough work with editing Marino (even when I was late delivering him).

Zee, thank you for your thorough work with proofreading Marino and for all of the encouragement as you were reading him.

To Jasmine and Casey, my PA's. I'm sorry I'm such a hot mess and I'm forever grateful that you put up with me!

Sophie!! You are a literal queen and I am so glad that I have you in my life, not only to read through Marino and convince me he's not a pile of crap, but also because your friendship is a gift I am blessed to have.

And finally, to my readers who have loved Bianchi, Dark Ties and Stolen Vows. You give me the push to keep doing this and I'll be eternally grateful for that.

About the Author

Addison Tate is an author of dark, intoxicating romances that blend passion, power, and a touch of danger. She also writes contemporary billionaire romance under the pen name *KA James*.

Based near London, UK, Addison has spent years working in HR, but her true love has always been storytelling. She wrote her first story at fourteen—a tragic tale where everyone met their demise—and has been writing love stories ever since.

She hopes you loved *Marino* and can't wait to share what's next in the series. Stay connected for exclusive updates, behind-the-scenes content, and new releases by following her on social media or subscribing to her newsletter.